FROM NANCY DREW'S CASEBOOK

ASSIGNMENT: To pose as a student, go undercover, and investigate a series of thefts at Bedford High.

CONTACT: Daryl Gray, a gorgeous senior with sexy, blueberry-colored eyes and an instant attraction to Nancy.

SUSPECTS: Jake Webb, a genuine creep who seems to have something on half the kids at school.

Walt "Hunk" Hogan, the tough football captain who's acting strangely paranoid.

Carla Dalton, who hates Nancy on sight. Mere jealousy—or something more sinister?

Hal Morgan, the class "brain" who Nancy catches cheating on a test.

COMPLICATIONS: There's more going on at this school than meets the eye. Much more. If Nancy isn't careful, she could get herself into serious trouble . . . She could get herself killed.

Books in THE NANCY DREW FILES® Series

Available from ARCHWAY paperbacks

THE NANCY DREW FILES™   CASE · 1

SECRETS CAN KILL

Carolyn Keene

AN ARCHWAY PAPERBACK
Published by POCKET BOOKS • NEW YORK

AN ARCHWAY PAPERBACK *Original*

An Archway Paperback published by
POCKET BOOKS, a division of Simon & Schuster, Inc.
1230 Avenue of the Americas, New York, N.Y. 10020

ISBN: 0-671-64193-X

First Archway Paperback printing August, 1986

10 9 8 7 6 5 4 3

NANCY DREW, AN ARCHWAY PAPERBACK and colophon
are registered trademarks of Simon & Schuster, Inc.

THE NANCY DREW FILES is a trademark
of Simon & Schuster, Inc.

Printed in U.S.A.

IL 7+

Chapter

One

HANDS ON HER hips, Nancy Drew stood in the middle of her bedroom and surveyed the situation. New clothes lay everywhere—strewn across the bed, draped over the backs of chairs, and spilling out of shopping bags.

Laughing at the mess, Nancy reached for a just-bought pair of designer jeans. "How do you like the new look in private detectives?" she said, slipping the jeans on. "Undercover and overdressed!"

"I'd give anything to have a job like yours." Bess Marvin studied the label on an oversized green sweater that would be perfect with

Nancy's reddish-blond hair. "Not only did you get to buy a whole closetful of clothes for it, but you'll probably be asked out by every good-looking boy at Bedford High."

George Fayne swallowed the last of her frozen yogurt and asked, "What's going on at that school, anyway?"

"I don't know all the details yet, but it doesn't sound too terrible," Nancy said. "Lockers broken into, a few files and some video equipment missing, stuff like that." She zipped up the jeans and took the sweater Bess was holding out. "The principal, Mr. Parton, said he'd tell me more tomorrow. I won't say the case is going to be a piece of cake," Nancy said with a grin, "but it doesn't exactly sound like the hardest sleuthing I've ever done, either."

At eighteen, Nancy Drew already had a reputation in her home town of River Heights as one of the brightest, hottest young detectives around. And she'd earned every bit of that reputation the hard way—by tracking down clues and solving mysteries that ranged from arson to kidnapping.

Nancy took every case seriously, of course, but somehow, going undercover as a high-school student to find a smalltime vandal just didn't seem very heavy. After all, she'd been up against some really tough characters in the past, like armed robbers and blackmailers.

Nancy studied herself in the mirror. She liked

what she saw. The tight jeans looked great on her long, slim legs and the green sweater complemented her strawberry-blond hair. Her eyes flashed with the excitement of a new case. She was counting on solving the little mystery fairly easily. In fact, Nancy thought it would probably be fun! "Right now," she said to her two friends, "the hardest part of this case is deciding what to wear."

"That outfit, definitely," Bess said, sighing with envy at Nancy's slender figure. "You'll make the guys absolutely drool."

"That's all she needs," George joked. "A bunch of freshmen following her around like underage puppies."

"Oh, yeah? Have you seen the captain of the Bedford football team?" Bess rolled her eyes. "They don't call him 'Hunk' Hogan for nothing!"

Bess and George were Nancy's best friends, and they were cousins, but that was about all they had in common. Blond-haired Bess was bubbly and easygoing, and always on the lookout for two things: a good diet and a great date. So far she hadn't found either. She was constantly trying to lose five pounds, and she fell in and out of love every other month.

George, with curly dark hair and a shy smile, was quiet, with a dry sense of humor and the beautifully toned body of an athlete. George liked boys as much as Bess did, but she was more serious about love. "When I fall," she'd say, "it's going to be for real."

Both girls had helped Nancy to solve cases in the past, and they'd just spent the entire day with her at the shopping mall, helping Bedford High's "new girl" choose her new wardrobe.

"Anyway," Bess went on, "Nancy will be completely immune to the charms of Hunk Hogan. She's got Ned, right, Nan?"

"Right." Nancy glanced at the mirror above her dresser, where she'd stuck a snapshot of Ned Nickerson, and her grin changed to a soft smile as she thought of the first boy she'd ever loved.

Nancy and Ned had a very special relationship. They'd known each other since they were kids, and when they'd first realized they loved each other, they'd thought it would last forever. But neither one was ready yet for a "forever" commitment, so occasionally they drifted apart, dating other people. Yet somehow, Nancy always found herself coming back to Ned. They were so in tune with each other that no matter what they were doing—whether it was tracking down the clues to a mystery or planning a private party for two—it seemed that they could read each other's thoughts.

Nancy smiled to herself and wondered if Ned knew what she was thinking at that moment, which was: that as good as he looked in a photograph, with his light brown hair, soft dark

4

eyes, and gently curving mouth, Ned was a hundred times better in the flesh.

Shivering as she remembered the feel of his arms around her, Nancy promised herself that when she solved the Bedford High case, she would definitely join him for a long weekend with his family at their cabin in the mountains.

"You're right," she said again. "In my eyes, no guy can compete with Ned. But if I meet some really gorgeous senior, I'll be sure to get his number for you."

"Great!" Bess fingered the gold locket she always wore around her neck. When she was in love, the locket carried a picture of the lucky boy. At the moment it was empty. "But I don't want to be a complete hog," she said with a laugh. "Get a number for George, too."

George blushed and tossed a pillow at her cousin. "No, thanks. I'll find my own guy."

"I've heard that before," Bess joked. "Come on, Nancy's in a perfect position to fix us up. Who knows when we'll have a chance like this again?"

George tossed a second pillow, but by then she was laughing, too. "Nancy's supposed to be solving a crime, not setting us up."

"Who cares? She can do both! Right, Nan?"

Bess tossed one of the pillows at Nancy, Nancy tossed it back, and in a few seconds, the girls were in the middle of a full-fledged pillow fight. Soon the room was a bigger mess than ever, as feathers flew from the pillows and slowly drifted down onto the piles of clothes and shopping bags.

The free-for-all was still going strong when the Drews' housekeeper stuck her head around the door and good-naturedly dodged a flying pillow.

Hannah Gruen had been with the Drews since Nancy was born. After Mrs. Drew died, when Nancy was still a baby, Hannah's role had grown way beyond that of housekeeper. Mrs. Gruen had hugged and scolded Nancy through childhood, bandaging scraped knees and kissing away tears. As the years went by, she was always ready with encouragement and advice. And, of course, the hugging and scolding had continued, too. In time Hannah had become almost a second mother to Nancy. She was always there when Nancy's father's work as a lawyer took him away from his daughter. Carson Drew trusted Hannah implicitly, and Nancy loved her without question.

"Hannah!" Nancy giggled when she saw Mrs. Gruen in the doorway. "I know what you're going to say—it's a school night, and I'd better clean up my room fast and get to bed early!"

"Well, I couldn't help thinking that you *are* starting a new assignment tomorrow, and you *should* probably get a good night's rest," Hannah said. "But the real reason I'm here is to give you this." She handed Nancy a bulky manila envelope.

Nancy took it and saw her name printed in black marker. There was no return address, no stamp, no postmark. "Where did this come from?" she asked.

"I haven't the vaguest idea," Hannah replied. "I went out to sweep the front porch about five minutes ago and there it was, poking out of the mailbox."

Nancy fingered the package, then held it up to her ear. "Well, it's not ticking," she joked.

She ripped open the envelope and pulled out an unlabeled videotape.

"Oh, terrific," Bess said. "A movie. I've been dying to see a good movie lately."

"Too bad we don't have any popcorn," George said as they trooped down the hall toward the den.

"I just bought a bag," Hannah said, heading for the kitchen. "Come help yourselves if you get hungry."

In the den Nancy turned on the television and then opened the cabinet that held the VCR. "I wish I knew where this came from," she said. "Who goes around leaving videotapes on peoples' doorsteps?"

"Maybe it's some advertising gimmick," Bess suggested.

"No, I've got it!" George began laughing.

"It's that workout tape Bess was so interested in—the one with all the gorgeous hunks."

Nancy grinned. "Yeah, I had the feeling she was more interested in the hunks than the exercises." She slipped the tape into the deck and pushed the play button. "Okay," she said, joining Bess and George on the couch, "get ready."

The girls were still laughing as the movie started, but after the first few seconds, the laughter stopped.

"What is this, anyway?" George asked.

Leaning forward from her corner of the couch, Bess gave a little cry of surprise. "It's *us*," she said. "Look!"

In silence the girls watched themselves doing exactly what they'd done six hours earlier: entering the shopping mall and arguing about which store to go to first.

But after that the camera stayed almost exclusively on Nancy. There she was, studying the mannequins in the window of a fashionable boutique; there she was again, coming out of a store called Ups & Downs, checking her pocketbook.

"You were afraid you'd left your credit card in the store," Bess said. "Remember?"

"I remember." Nancy didn't take her eyes off the screen. "But I don't remember anybody hanging around with a video camera, taping the whole thing."

The tape stayed on Nancy: riding the escalator, going in and out of stores, sipping a Coke. Then it showed the three friends eating hotdogs by the fountain in the center of the mall.

"It's true," Bess remarked, "the camera does add ten pounds."

George shook her head. "This has to be some kind of weird joke."

"It's weird, all right," Nancy agreed. "But if it's a joke, I'm not laughing."

"There can't be much more," Bess said. "Panache was the last store we went into."

Sure enough, as they watched themselves come out of Panache, the camera zoomed in on Nancy. The last frame froze in a close-up of her smiling face.

Nancy was reaching out to turn off the tape machine when a screeching, whining sound made her stop, her hand in midair.

Then a high-pitched, hideously shrieking voice invaded the Drews' cozy den. "Stick with shopping, Nancy Drew. It's a lot safer than snooping at Bedford High!"

Chapter

Two

EARLY THE NEXT morning, as Nancy was pulling her red Mustang out of the Drews' driveway, the sound of the frightening voice came back to her once again. "Stick to shopping, huh?" Nancy muttered under her breath. "Fat chance." She shifted her car into drive and was just stepping on the gas when she saw Hannah hurrying out the front door.

"You almost forgot this," Hannah said, handing Nancy an orange canvas duffel bag that held notebooks, pens, and makeup—everything Nancy had packed for her "first day" at school.

"Thanks, Hannah." Nancy stifled a yawn and

smiled as she took the bag. "I almost forgot my most important prop for this job."

"You don't look very alert this morning, I must say," Hannah commented. "In fact, you look downright sleepy."

"I'm fine, Hannah, really. See you later!" Nancy waved cheerfully as she drove from her house, but Hannah had been right. Nancy was definitely less than bright-eyed and bushytailed.

No wonder, Nancy thought. Getting to sleep the night before had been next to impossible. She was always a little edgy before she started a new case, but the past night had been worse than usual. She'd lain awake, running the mysterious videotape through her mind over and over again.

The creepiest part was that horrible voice. The sound of it had echoed in Nancy's head all night and into the morning. It had obviously been electronically distorted, but realizing that didn't make it any less scary. And knowing that someone had been following her all day was definitely frightening. Nancy couldn't help thinking about the video equipment that had been taken from Bedford High. Could there be any link between the two? Nancy wondered.

Who was responsible? And why? Why would some high school kid who was into rifling lockers and stealing a few files go to such trouble to scare her off? And how did whoever it was know about Nancy's assignment? That was the question which had kept the young detective awake the longest.

Nancy had tried not to think about those pieces to the Bedford High puzzle. She knew she wouldn't figure them out until she actually got to the school campus and did some on-the-spot research. Still, she hadn't been able to keep her mind off the troubling questions. And there she was on the first day of a case, nervous and droopy-eyed!

As she drove the fifteen miles from River Heights to the town of Bedford, Nancy tuned the car radio to her favorite rock station, hoping the music would clear her head. She slowed, passing the local Ford dealer. The new Mustang GT Convertible she'd been drooling over was still inside. *Be cool, Nancy,* she said to herself with a half-smile, trying to keep her heart from pounding. Then, pressing her foot to the accelerator, she zoomed toward town.

Bedford was beautiful, small, but with large homes surrounded by lush lawns, and, no doubt, swimming pools tucked away in the back somewhere. On the outskirts of town, along the road to the high school, Nancy passed several houses that could only be described as mansions.

Bedford was obviously a place where a lot of

rich people lived, Nancy thought as she pulled up to a stoplight near the high school. At just that moment a sleek, expensive black Porsche 911 eased up beside her in the next lane.

Nancy glanced over, admiring the car, and its owner gently revved the engine. The powerful motor gave a soft, throaty rumble, then another. Nancy smiled at the obvious come-on and lifted her gaze to the driver.

The guy in the Porsche was one of the most gorgeous boys Nancy had ever seen. He looked about seventeen. He'd probably been a towhead when he was little, but now his blond hair was highlighted with streaks of honey-brown. And his eyes—were they brown or black?—were full of light and laughter as he gave Nancy a playful grin and revved the engine once more.

Suddenly Nancy was wide awake. She grinned back and fluttered the gas pedal on the Mustang. *Two can play this game,* she thought.

Out of the corner of her eye, Nancy saw the turn arrow change to green. Still looking at the boy, she smoothly shifted gears. Then she peeled out ahead of the Porsche, swinging wide into his lane so that he had to follow her all the way down Bedford Road. She was definitely back in high school!

Nancy lost sight of the Porsche somewhere in Bedford High's student parking lot, and as she joined the crowd of kids swarming up the school's front steps, she stopped thinking about it. Of course, its driver wasn't quite so easy to forget.

Bedford High wasn't big, with a total enrollment of about six hundred students. But it seemed to Nancy as if every one of those students was milling around in the building's big front hall. They looked like a typical bunch of kids. While they waited for the final bell, they laughed together, calling to each other, talking about dates and upcoming tests.

For a moment Nancy felt exactly like what she was pretending to be—a transfer student coming into a new school in the middle of fall semester. There she was, facing a bunch of strangers who already knew each other and were checking her out, trying to figure out who the new girl was. She felt exposed and self-conscious, and like all new kids, she wished she had a friend nearby. *That's the way you're supposed to feel,* Nancy told herself. At least it was a good cover.

Nancy was standing alone, trying to remember the directions to the principal's office that she had been given, when a snatch of conversation caught her attention.

"You know I can't give you a ride," a boy's voice said. Nancy could detect the frantic pleading in it. "I just *can't.* If I miss practice, I'll be kicked off the team!"

Then came a second boy's voice, calm and

slow and coldly self-assured. "Miss practice . . . or else," it ordered.

Nancy craned her neck, trying to locate the source of that unpleasant little exchange. There was no way, however, to match the voices to any of the faces in the mass of chattering students around her.

I guess there's at least one super-creep in every high school, Nancy thought to herself. But as she headed for the principal's office, she kept hearing the harsh sound of that calm, cold voice. There was an intimidating power in it. And obviously, whomever it belonged to had someone scared!

Nancy turned down one of Bedford High's drab green hallways. No matter how much high schools changed, she decided, the paint jobs never seemed to. Nancy found the principal's office and told the secretary that she had an appointment with Mr. Parton. The principal didn't keep Nancy waiting five seconds.

Stepping into the office, Nancy took one look at Mr. Parton and decided to try to solve this case in record time. Not only did she want that weekend with Ned, but Mr. Parton looked like he was on the verge of a nervous breakdown. For the sake of his health, she'd better work fast!

"It's driving me insane!" Mr. Parton declared, dramatically pounding his fists against his temples. "And are the police any help?

Noooo. Beef up security, they say. Ha! Try getting the salary for another guard out of the school board. A patrol car drives around the school every night. We can't be bothered with a little file-filching. It's your problem, they say."

Mr. Parton paused for breath and then chuckled to himself, shaking his bald head and smiling at Nancy with worried brown eyes. "Thank heavens I know your father. If he hadn't suggested that I hire you, I don't know what I'd have done."

Probably collapsed, Nancy told herself, but she kept her thoughts silent. She smiled. "I'm glad you did call me, Mr. Parton. I'm ready to get started, but first I just want to make sure I've got the facts straight. You mentioned files being taken. What files?"

"Actually, we're not sure." Mr. Parton shook his head again. "But my file cabinet and the senior guidance counselor's—both of which are kept locked, by the way—have been tampered with several times. We don't know if anything's missing because everything's always put back in the wrong place.

"Then there are the lockers," Mr. Parton went on, rubbing one hand over his shiny head. "We know that at least four lockers have been broken into. Our maintenance man reported them." He leaned forward, hands clasped. "But no students complained."

"It could have something to do with drugs,"

Nancy suggested. "That would explain why the kids kept their mouths shut."

"True. And I won't say that Bedford High is drug-free. But I do know for sure that there aren't any drugs in my file cabinet. And what about the school video equipment?"

Right, Nancy thought, remembering the "movie" she'd received.

"Whoever's taking the stuff is very selective," the principal said. "We lose a lens here, a battery pack there, then a couple of blank tapes. Some of it's even turned up mysteriously a few days after disappearing."

"And you're sure whoever's pulling all these stunts is one person?" Nancy asked.

"I'm not sure of anything," Mr. Parton said, frustration mounting in his voice. "But I'm almost certain that a student, or more than one student, is behind it all."

"Why couldn't it be a teacher?"

"Well, the police, much as I'm disappointed in them, did do me one favor. They questioned the faculty, checked them out, and came up with zilch, except for the bio teacher, who turned out to be a scofflaw. Two hundred dollars in unpaid parking tickets."

Nancy laughed. "Well, having me pose as a student was a good idea." She stood up and reached for her canvas bag. "I'd like to get started, but first I need to know if I have your permission to check things out my own way. I mean, I may have to break a few rules to get to the bottom of this."

"Whatever it takes. I'll clear it with the police," Mr. Parton said emphatically. "And don't go yet." He motioned for Nancy to sit again. "I may not be thinking too clearly these days, but I do know that you'll need a contact while you're here, somebody you can talk to freely. Someone who can introduce you to a lot of kids. The principal isn't going to help any student fit in. Even I know that."

"Your thinking's not all that fuzzy, Mr. Parton." Nancy laughed again. "So. Who's my contact?"

"One of our seniors. A good student, completely trustworthy. And very popular, president of the class, which is why I chose him. He can get you in touch with all the various 'crowds.'"

"You mean he knows about me already?" Nancy asked, once again thinking about the videotape.

"No, I thought I'd introduce you two and let him in on the plan at the same time." Mr. Parton checked his watch. "He should be here any minute."

At that moment there was a knock at the door. Mr. Parton opened it, and Nancy looked up and found herself face to face with the beautiful driver of the black Porsche!

"Nancy Drew," the principal said, "meet Daryl Gray."

His eyes weren't brown or black, Nancy noticed immediately. They were the dark, dusky color of ripe blueberries, and they were rimmed with lashes that had to be at least half an inch long. Nancy had never seen eyes like that in her life.

Some contact! she thought.

Daryl Gray listened politely and with interest as Mr. Parton explained the entire situation. If he was surprised at Nancy's role, he didn't show it.

Instead, Daryl's incredible eyes kept straying to Nancy each time Mr. Parton mentioned her name. And when the principal said something about Daryl showing Nancy the ropes, Daryl's mouth curved into a slow, teasing grin. Nancy couldn't help returning it.

The attraction between them crackled like electricity. Nancy wondered how Mr. Parton could possibly miss the sparks, but he seemed oblivious to everything but his problem. He went on and on. As Nancy tuned out the principal's voice, she tuned into the beautiful face before her.

Finally the harried principal said something that brought Nancy back to reality. "Nancy, the school is counting on you. I've done what I can. Now it's up to you. At this moment Daryl is the only one, aside from me, who knows who you are and what you're doing here. The rest is in your hands."

And Nancy, remembering that hideous voice on the tape, finally tore her eyes away from Daryl. *You're wrong, Mr. Parton*, she thought. *Somebody else knows who I am. And that's the person I have to find!*

Chapter

Three

THE WARNING BELL rang just as Nancy and Daryl left Mr. Parton's office. Together they fell into step with the crowd of kids hurrying to their homeroom classes. Out of the corner of her eye Nancy caught Daryl looking at her, a strange little smile on his lips. "What's funny?" she asked.

"Nothing." Daryl laughed softly and shook his head. "It's just that I've never met a detective, especially a beautiful redhead who drives a Mustang."

Nancy laughed too. "Well, I've never met a senior who drives a Porsche."

"It's my favorite toy." They rounded a corner

and Daryl casually put his hand on Nancy's shoulder to guide her out of the way of a group of kids coming in the opposite direction. "I'll have to give you a ride sometime, show you what it can do."

At the touch of Daryl's hand, Nancy felt a delicious tingling sensation, and suddenly she found herself wondering what it would be like to have Daryl's arms around her. Daryl Gray was a powerfully attractive guy.

"Do you think it would be good for making fast getaways?" Nancy went on in the same teasing manner.

"Sure," Daryl replied, leaving his hand where it was, "but I hope you're not planning to make a getaway real soon. After all, we just met."

"And besides, I have a mystery to solve, remember?"

"Right. And I hope it takes a long, long time."

They were both laughing, looking into each other's eyes as they turned another corner and bumped into what felt to Nancy like a rock wall.

"Sorry," the wall said.

Nancy touched her nose to make sure it wasn't broken, and then smiled at the guy, who was big and handsome, and built like a truck.

"Walt, meet Nancy Drew. She's a transfer student," Daryl said smoothly. "Nancy, Walt Hogan."

Nancy smiled again, remembering what Bess had said about Bedford's football captain. "Hunk" fit him perfectly.

"Yeah," Walt said, not returning her smile, "nice to meet you."

Walt strode off, and Nancy turned to Daryl. "He seemed a little angry," she commented.

"Yeah, he hasn't been Mr. Friendly lately," Daryl agreed. "And you should see him in action on the field. He's like a bear just out of hibernation—mean and hungry."

"I don't suppose he's a video freak, by any chance?"

"I thought detectives were supposed to be more subtle than that."

"Why should I be subtle with you?" Nancy teased. "You're my contact, aren't you?"

Daryl's hand tightened on Nancy's shoulder. "I sure am," he said softly.

Nancy and Daryl were standing in front of Nancy's homeroom class, waiting for the final bell to ring. About ten other kids were waiting, too, and as Nancy laughed at Daryl's last remark, she caught a girl staring at them.

The girl was blond, pretty in a tough, hard-edged kind of way, but she didn't look too friendly, Nancy thought. She was watching Daryl intently. Then as someone called out "Carla!" she moved her eyes to Nancy's face for just a second before turning away. In that brief instant she gave Nancy the strangest look. It

23

wasn't a look of dislike, Nancy thought, it was more like a challenge. She wondered how much this Carla knew about her.

The final bell rang, and Daryl gave Nancy's shoulder another squeeze. "I guess this is it for now," he said. He leaned so close that Nancy felt his breath on her ear. "You're on your own, detective."

Actually, Nancy didn't expect to do much detecting on her first day. She was new in school; she had to find her way around, get used to the rhythm of the place, and meet a few people before she could start asking questions.

Part of Nancy's cover was to act like a new girl—lost and a little out of it—which was easy, since that was how she felt. Daryl wasn't in any of her classes and she didn't know anyone else.

Most of the kids ignored Nancy. The first really friendly girl she met was a pretty blond with aquamarine eyes, who waylaid Nancy after English.

"Hi, I'm Sara Ames," she said. "You're new here, aren't you?"

"My name's Nancy Drew, and you're right, I'm brand-new."

"Well, don't worry, you'll fit in fast," Sara said. "But I wanted to get to you before anybody else did."

"Oh?" Nancy wondered if Sara might have some secret information.

"I'm editor of the *Bedford Sentinel*," Sara went on, "and we're desperate for people to work on the paper. I noticed in English that you can at least read and write," she joked. "And I bet you're going to be popular, so you'll have lots of good contacts. The *Sentinel*'s fun. What do you think?"

Nancy smiled to herself at the thought of her "contact." She smiled at Sara, too, for making her feel welcomed. "Thanks for asking," she said. "Let me feel my way around a little more, okay? Then I'll let you know."

"Great! There's a staff meeting tonight, room 215. I hope you can make it." With a friendly wave, Sara dashed down the hall.

Nancy's next class was American history. She'd almost forgotten just how boring a bad teacher could be, but the droning voice, the intimidating looks, all of it reminded her why she'd been happy to leave high school behind. She'd certainly be happy to leave history behind! The forty-five minute period dragged on and on. Halfway through, Nancy let her mind wander. Anything was better than the teacher's monotone!

Purposely putting Bedford High's mystery out of her mind, Nancy thought about Sara Ames's offer to join the newspaper staff. She was tempted to accept it. Maybe she could have a double cover—new girl and student reporter, investigating the vandal of Bedford High. It might work, she thought. But once she solved the case, she'd be leaving the school, and that would leave Sara minus one reporter. It didn't seem fair.

When American history was finally over, Nancy heaved a sigh of relief along with the rest of the students. "Class," the teacher called over the noise of the final bell, "read the next two chapters in your textbook for homework."

"Great," Nancy groaned to herself. "Boring homework, too." The Bedford High mystery was turning out to have hidden liabilities!

On the way to lunch Nancy spotted Sara Ames at the entrance to the cafeteria and decided to tell her she wouldn't be joining the newspaper. That way Sara wouldn't feel hurt when Nancy didn't show up at the staff meeting.

"Hi," Nancy said. "Listen, thanks for asking me to join the paper, but I think I'd better make sure my grades are in good enough shape before I do anything else, you know?"

"Okay," said Sara. "I understand. Just let me know whenever you're ready."

"Thanks," said Nancy.

Sara rushed off, and Nancy entered the cafeteria. She looked around uncertainly. Where should she sit?

At that moment she heard someone call her name. Turning, she saw Connie Watson waiting in the cafeteria line.

Nancy knew Connie's name because the

teacher had called on her in French class. Connie's face had turned the color of a ripe tomato as she'd given her answer, and after class Nancy had noticed that no one walked out of the room with her. Connie was slightly pudgy, but her eyes, though anxious and a little fearful, were friendly. She smiled shyly and said, "Hey, would you like to eat lunch with me?"

"I wish I could," Nancy said sincerely, "but I've got to talk to the counselor about my schedule—I've been stuck with two gym classes, can you believe it? I'm just going to grab a yogurt and keep going!"

What Nancy really wanted was a chance to snoop around the video lab, providing it was empty. If it wasn't, maybe she could ask a few "innocent" questions.

After promising Connie that she'd sit with her the next day, Nancy paid for her yogurt, headed down the hall, turned a corner, and stopped. *Some detective you are,* she told herself. *You didn't even bother to find out where the video lab is!*

Nancy was about ready to go back to the cafeteria and ask Connie when she saw Carla walking toward her. Nancy hadn't forgotten the challenging look Carla had given her that morning, but she put on a bright smile anyway. "Hi. This is embarrassing, but I'm lost. Could you point me in the direction of the video lab?"

"Oh, it's easy to get lost in this place," Carla said with a friendly smile. "Just go to the end of this hall, turn left and follow the hall to the end. Then go through the door on your right and down the stairs. You can't miss it."

"Thanks," Nancy said, just as nicely. "I appreciate it."

Maybe I was just being paranoid this morning, she thought as she walked along. Nancy turned left and went down the second hall. She pushed open the door, started down the steps, and stopped. The staircase obviously wasn't going to take her to the video lab. From the look of things, it would probably lead straight to the boiler room.

On the other hand, she thought, *maybe Carla really is a prime pain in the you-know-what.*

Or maybe Carla had something to do with the anonymous videotape. That might explain why she would go out of her way to steer Nancy away from the video lab.

Nancy was moving back up the stairs when she heard scuffling sounds from below. She stopped, listening, then heard a muffled shout.

"Just lay off, Jake," a voice said. "I've given you what you want, so get off my back." The voice grew angrier. "You're a nobody, Webb, a real waste of space. Why don't you make like a ghost and vanish?"

Footsteps pounded up the stairs. Before Nancy could move, Walt Hogan, the surly star of the football team, was beside her. He wasn't just surly, though. He was furious, his face flushed with anger. Walt shouldered Nancy roughly aside. Then his fury exploded and he rammed his clenched fists into the door before shoving it open and storming through.

While Nancy tried to decide whether to run after Walt, she heard a soft laugh. Looking down, she saw another boy, one she hadn't met before, staring up at her.

"Well, if it isn't Bedford High's newest scholar, Nancy Drew," the boy sneered. "I'm Jake Webb."

Jake smiled as he began climbing the stairs toward Nancy, but the look in his eyes was cold. "Do you always go around poking your nose into other people's business?" he asked. "Not too nice, Nancy Drew. Maybe I ought to explain a few rules to you. Otherwise, you won't get very far at Bedford High."

Nancy recognized the voice. It was the same one she'd heard in the main hall that morning, coolly ordering some desperate kid to "miss practice—or else." Jake's face went with his voice, Nancy thought—lean and bony, with a tight-lipped smile under sharp, ice-blue eyes.

Nancy felt an overwhelming urge to tell the creep to buzz off. But Jake wasn't acting like the average high-school egomaniac, and she was curious to see what he was up to.

Jake climbed the stairs until his eyes were

level with Nancy's. Still smiling, he ran one finger lazily up her arm, across her neck, and to her lips.

"Rule One," Jake said softly. "Keep your mouth shut about what you just heard. If you don't, you'll never learn Rule Two."

Chapter

Four

NANCY WAS TEMPTED to bite Jake's finger and see what happened, but instead she forced herself to push his hand away calmly. She was so furious, she didn't even think about being frightened. Who did this guy think he was, anyway?

"Who makes these rules?" she asked. "You, I suppose?"

"Clever Nancy," Jake said with a laugh. "Go to the head of the class."

The longer Nancy stood there, the stronger the urge she had to push Jake Webb down the stairs. She'd already decided that he was a prime candidate for the Bedford High vandal (not to mention the Bedford town jail), but at the moment all she wanted was to get rid of him.

"Look," she said, "I don't know what you're trying to do, but I think I ought to tell you that I don't scare easily." She put her hand on the door. "Why don't you just crawl back under your rock?"

Without waiting for Jake's reaction, Nancy pulled the door open and almost bumped into Daryl Gray.

"Well, well," Jake scoffed. "It's 'King Cool.'"

Completely ignoring Jake, Daryl smiled at Nancy. "Hi. I expected to see you in the cafeteria."

"She couldn't make it," Jake said. "She had more important things to do than eat."

"You okay?" Daryl asked Nancy.

"I was getting a little bored with the company, but I'm fine now," she said. "How'd you know I was here?"

"Are you kidding?" Jake leaned against the doorjamb and grinned. "King Cool has the inside track on everything—girls, cars, clever ways to make money. Right, King?"

Quickly Daryl shifted his glance to Jake. "You talk too much, Webb," he said sharply. "I'm tired of the sound of your voice. Do everybody a favor and give your mouth a rest."

"Anything you say, King." Jake held Daryl's

gaze for a second. "But my eyes'll still be open—you can count on that." Then he slouched off down the hall.

Nancy let out her breath. "What was all that business about your money and keeping his eyes open?"

"Hard to tell with that guy," Daryl said. "How'd you run into him, anyway?"

Nancy explained, and noticed a funny look on Daryl's face when she mentioned Carla, but she decided not to ask about it. "Anyway, I'm glad you came along," she said. "I was just about ready to blow my cover with that creep."

"Jake Webb's personality fits his name," Daryl said with a grimace. "He's just like a spider waiting for a fly to come along. I can't believe he actually works in the principal's office. But most of us here aren't candidates for the psycho ward like he is. I'll prove it to you if you'll come to the dance with me this weekend."

"That's a pretty intriguing invitation," Nancy said with a coy smile. "I'm too curious to turn you down."

"It's a date, then."

Daryl touched her arm in a familiar gesture before walking away. Once again, Nancy thrilled to the feel of his hand. As she hurried to her next class, she pictured the two of them dancing together, arms around each other. The picture brought a smile to her face. As long as she was at Bedford High, she thought, she might as well have some fun. And Daryl Gray was the perfect person to have it with.

By the time her last class of the day was over, Nancy's head was a blur of names and faces, a jumble of bells and pounding feet. As she'd expected, she hadn't done much detecting at all. Only two people—Carla and Jake—stood out in her mind as possibly connected to the vandalism and to the videotape she'd received.

She wanted to find out more about both of them, but first she wanted to take a look around the video lab to see if she could discover any connection between the missing equipment and the mysterious tape.

She wasn't taking any chances on getting lost a second time—she asked a teacher for directions and, after stashing some books in her locker, made her way to room 235.

The door was locked. *Probably only the teacher has a key.* Well, Mr. Parton *had* given her permission to do "whatever it takes," she thought. She reached into her duffel bag and pulled out an extremely handy little device—a credit card—and took a careful look down the hall.

Connie Watson was walking straight toward her.

"Hi, Nancy!" Connie called. "I've been looking for you. The football team's got practice this afternoon and I thought you might want to go to it with me." Connie blushed and bit her lip. "You don't have to, though. I mean, if you're too busy, that's okay," she said quickly, as if she were used to being rejected.

"No, I think I'd like that," Nancy said, pocketing the credit card. Maybe she'd get a chance to talk to Walt Hogan. She was very curious about the cryptic conversation she'd overheard on the stairs. "Let's go."

The weather was warm for early October, and several dozen kids were sitting in the bleachers watching the players and the cheerleading squad. Nancy and Connie arrived just in time to see Hunk Hogan getting chewed out royally by the coach. Nancy couldn't hear what was being said, but she wondered if Walt was in trouble because he'd arrived late. If that was it, then it was probably his voice she'd heard in the main hall that morning, pleading with Jake. She hadn't recognized it when she met him, but if it *was* Walt, then she had more reason than ever to talk to him.

The cheerleaders were energetic and colorful in their bright orange and white uniforms. Nancy admired their routines and even had to admit that Carla, who seemed to be the captain, was very good.

Beside her, Connie sighed. "I'd give anything

to be a cheerleader," she confided. "Of course, I'm too fat, so it's not worth thinking about. Besides, even if I were skinny, I'd never make it. Not with Carla Dalton in charge. She can't stand me."

Nancy nodded sympathetically. "She's not too crazy about me, either, but I don't have a clue why."

"Oh, that's easy," Connie said. "Ever since you arrived at Bedford High, Daryl Gray hasn't taken his eyes off of you, and Carla can't stand competition." She put her hand over her mouth and giggled. "Personally, I love seeing Carla get what she deserves."

"You mean Carla and Daryl have a thing going?" Nancy asked. That explained the funny look on Daryl's face when Carla's name had been mentioned. Nancy couldn't picture Daryl being interested in someone like that, but she really didn't know him all that well.

"Off and on," Connie told her. "It's been off for a couple of weeks, but when you showed up, I guess Carla decided you were invading her territory."

So Carla's jealous, Nancy thought. That might make her nasty, but it didn't make her a criminal.

"Actually, I'm surprised she still wants Daryl," Connie went on. "Carla's only interested in one thing—money."

"Well, Daryl can't be heading for the poorhouse," Nancy remarked. "Not if he drives around in a Porsche."

"It is a little weird," Connie agreed, "especially since his father lost practically all his money a few months ago in some big business fiasco. For a while the Grays were one of the richest families in Bedford, but now . . ."

Connie's voice trailed off as she shook her head in sympathy. Nancy was sympathetic, too, but she was also curious. Not about the Grays' money problems—that was simply none of her business—but about what other tidbits of information Connie might have. She was something of a gossip, Nancy thought, and gossips could be a big help. Connie was chattering away again, pointing out various kids on the field, when Nancy noticed the bracelet on her right wrist. "That's beautiful," she said, touching it. "What is it, art deco?"

"I . . . I don't know," Connie said nervously fingering the intricately patterned gold. "It was a present . . . I don't know anything about jewelry."

"I love it. It looks like an antique," Nancy told her. A little flattery never hurt when you wanted information, and besides, she really liked Connie. "So, tell me more about Bedford High," she prompted. "Hey, I hear there're some weird things going on—stuff getting stolen and lockers broken into."

"You must mean the 'phantom,'" Connie

said, seeming relieved at the change in subject. "That's what I call him, since no one knows who he is."

"Got any ideas?"

"No. And most kids don't really care. I mean, it's all so juvenile."

So much for inside information. Then Nancy had to sit on the hard bleachers for an hour as Connie proceeded to give her a detailed account of everyone's love life, grades, family, and friends. Nancy learned a lot, but nothing that was going to help. One day down, she thought. How many more to go?

Nancy arrived at school the next day, determined to start putting the puzzle together, or at least to gather a few of the pieces.

Instead of study hall she had gym during second period, and stretching her muscles and limbering up felt good. Maybe the exercise would limber her mind up, too, so she could solve the case.

Two minutes into gym, though, her mind was on something else.

"Excuse me," a voice said.

Nancy stopped in the middle of a sit-up and smiled at Carla Dalton, who was standing over her. Who knows, she thought, maybe a smile would help.

"I'd really appreciate it," Carla said, "if you'd keep your problems to yourself."

"What are you talking about?"

Carla put a hand on her cocked hip. "I'm talking about the way you ran and tattled to Daryl yesterday," she said nastily. "He chewed me out about it this morning. I mean, can't you fight your own battles?"

"Let's get something straight," Nancy said calmly. "I didn't 'tattle' to Daryl. He asked me how I got lost, and I told him. I don't want to fight with you, Carla," she went on, "but since you asked, yes, I can fight my own battles—and I usually win."

Nancy went back to her sit-ups, still smiling, but inside she was seething. *This is all I need,* she thought, *a cat fight.*

A few minutes later, though, she wondered just how petty the cat fight was going to be. It was her turn on the trampoline, and as she prepared to go into a high flip, she noticed that the girl spotting her had changed places—with Carla Dalton.

It threw her concentration off. It shouldn't have, but it did. And as she sprung high into the air, she knew she was off balance.

There was no time to catch herself. If she'd had a reliable person spotting her, she wouldn't have worried, but Carla's back, she noticed, was conveniently turned. Before Nancy could stop herself, she was hurtling over the end of the trampoline—heading for a major collision with the floor!

Chapter

Five

Aᴛ ᴛʜᴇ ʟᴀsᴛ possible second, Nancy pushed her body to the limit, twisted desperately in midair, and hit the floor—with her rear end. Thank goodness not with her head. It wasn't the most graceful move she'd ever made, but as she sat there breathing shakily, she decided that it was better to be a klutz than a corpse.

Nancy was tempted to prove to Carla then and there that she was ready to fight the battle. But when she got to her feet, she noticed that the gym teacher was doing it for her.

"Dalton!" Miss Gibbs was livid. "This isn't the pom-pom squad. You have to use your brains in here, if you have any! Drew could have broken her neck!"

Which would not have broken Carla's heart, Nancy thought grimly. It would have made her day.

Most of the girls had rushed over to Nancy, asking if she was all right, whether she needed to see the nurse, whether she was sure nothing was broken.

"Thanks," Nancy said gratefully. "I'm still in one piece. But I think I lost something."

"What?" somebody asked.

"An inch off my hips," Nancy joked. "It's permanently embedded in the gym floor!"

Twenty minutes later, Nancy took her seat in social studies. She was still slightly rattled and was hoping for a lecture so she could just take notes and get her breath back.

"Okay," the teacher said gleefully, "clear your desks of everything but paper and pen. It's pop-quiz time!"

Nancy joined the other kids in groaning, and took as long as possible finding a notebook and pen.

"Don't worry," the boy behind her said. "Mr. Warner's quizzes are so bad, nobody passes. If you flunk, you won't be alone."

"Right," the girl to her left said. "The only one with a chance is Hal Morgan."

Nancy glanced to her right and noticed that

Hal Morgan was chewing his fingernails nervously.

"He doesn't look too confident," she whispered.

"Yeah, that's weird," the girl whispered back. "You know, it's funny. Hal's been the class brain forever. Always studying, you know? Never had time for anything else. But then this September, he surprised everybody by running for class president against Daryl Gray. He didn't win, but he sure did try. I can't believe how much time he spent campaigning."

"Maybe that's why he looks nervous," Nancy said. "Maybe his grades dropped during the campaign."

The girl shrugged. "Maybe. But he's been talking about going to Harvard, so he must be doing something right. And his SATs were off the top of the scale."

"Okay, scholars," Mr. Warner cackled. "Let's get this show on the road!"

By the fifth question, Nancy had decided that the boy behind her was right. There was no way she was going to pass the quiz. At least she didn't have to worry about her grade-point average, like everybody else.

She glanced at the clock, to see how much more torture she might have to go through. As she did she noticed that Hal Morgan seemed to be having trouble concentrating, too. In fact, his eyes were on *Nancy's* paper. As soon as he saw her glance at him, he looked away.

The teacher asked the next question, and Nancy wrote down her answer. Then she deliberately put her hands to her hair so her paper would be clear.

Sure enough, Hal made a pretense of stretching and yawning, and as he rolled his head around, his eyes once more zeroed in on Nancy's paper.

It was obvious, to Nancy anyway, that Hal the Brain was copying her answers. But why? Why would somebody so smart bother to cheat on a pop quiz?

Well, it sure isn't going to do him any good, she thought as they passed their papers to the front. *Hal's going to get exactly what I get, which is probably a fifty.*

She didn't think much more of the incident until after class. As she left the room, she saw Jake Webb lurking in the hall. Then she saw Hal walk up to him, reluctantly, the way most people walk into a dentist's office.

Wondering what those two could possibly have in common, Nancy attached herself to a group of kids who were standing around, moaning about the quiz.

It was hard to hear everything, but she caught enough to make her extremely curious.

"Listen," Hal was saying, "I've got my own essay to write before I can get to yours!"

"That's cool," Jake said. "I'll give you till tomorrow. How's that?"

"That's not enough time, and you know it." Hal sounded panicky.

"Oh, too bad," said Jake sarcastically. "Well, I guess I don't have to tell you what'll happen, right?"

Hal let out a big sigh and Nancy saw the defeated look on his face. "Okay, okay," he said. "You'll have it tomorrow."

That guy is really the pits, Nancy thought as she watched Jake walk cockily down the hall. *He acts like a king, and he's got at least two lackeys—Walt and Hal—doing his bidding. How many others are hustling to follow his orders? And why? Why would anyone want to do anything for Jake Webb?*

Without really thinking about it, Nancy had begun following Jake, but when she saw him turn into another hall and open his locker, she decided she might learn something about him if she could see what was inside that locker. She didn't know what she'd be looking for—money, maybe—but it was worth a try.

As she passed him she got a look at the locker number—515—and before Jake saw her, she walked quickly to the water fountain at the end of the hall. She had to drink enough to float a ship, but finally she saw Jake's scuffed sneakers pass by and out of sight.

It was lunch time and the hall was empty.

Nancy moved quickly to locker 515. A credit card wouldn't be any help this time. But a professional lock-picker's kit would. Fortunately, along with her makeup and lunch money, Nancy's canvas bag just happened to have such a kit. She found the right-size pick and had the padlock off in half a minute. She pulled the door open and was ready for a leisurely exploration when she heard a voice.

"Be back in a second," it said, "I forgot my psych book."

It was Jake Webb. Quickly Nancy raked her eyes over the inside of his locker. Only one thing caught her attention—a shoebox. Dangling from it was a beautiful gold bracelet, *exactly* like Connie Watson's.

That was all Nancy had time for. She shut the door and moved away just as she heard Jake's footsteps round the corner.

He has no way of knowing what you were up to, she told herself. *Just keep on going.*

Nancy kept on going, but she was sure Jake Webb's eyes were on her back every step of the way.

She was glad to get out of his sight, even though once she was, Nancy still couldn't relax. What was Connie's bracelet doing in a shoebox in Jake Webb's locker? It had to be the same bracelet; it was an antique, probably one of a kind. Maybe Connie lost it and Jake, lowlife that he was, found it and decided to stash it.

When Nancy spotted Connie in the lunch line she decided to make sure she was right. "Hi," she said. "Guess what? I think I know where your bracelet is!"

Connie jumped as if she'd been stung. "My—my bracelet?"

Nancy pointed to Connie's bare wrist. "Right. You lost it, didn't you?"

Connie nodded, her eyes wide.

"Well," Nancy went on, "I'm pretty sure I saw it—are you ready?—in Jake Webb's locker!"

Shaking her head, Connie backed away slowly, fear in her eyes. "It—it couldn't be mine," she stammered. "I lost mine at home. I mean, I didn't lose it. I just didn't wear it today, that's all."

"Connie, what's wrong?"

"Nothing!" the frightened girl said. "Really, nothing's wrong! I have to go. There's this meeting I forgot about. I have to go," she said again, and all but ran away.

Some really weird things are going on at Bedford High, Nancy thought as she watched Connie hurry off. *And so far, they all lead to one person—Jake Webb.* She didn't know if Jake was the phantom vandal, or the anonymous videotaper. But she did know he was up to something. All she had to do was find out what.

* * *

By the end of the day Nancy was ready to explode. First Connie had treated her as if she had some horrible communicable disease. Then she couldn't find Walt Hogan or Hal Morgan, so she hadn't been able to question them. Plus, her rear end still ached from that fall off the trampoline. Things were definitely not going well. What she wanted most of all was to go home and soak in a hot tub.

Instead, Nancy decided she'd better make another pass at the video lab. She didn't want to leave Bedford High empty-handed, not for the second day in a row.

The lab wasn't locked. When Nancy walked in, the only person there was Daryl Gray, who was peering at a shelf of tapes. Suddenly she felt happy for the first time all day.

"Am I glad to see you!" she cried.

Daryl spun around, startled. Then his lips parted in his Porsche-driver's grin. "Nancy Drew, isn't it? New girl and"—he glanced around at the otherwise empty room—"private eye? How's the detecting going?"

"Don't ask," Nancy said with a groan. "Anyway, what are you doing here? I didn't know you belonged to the video club."

"I don't," Daryl said. "I was just doing some detecting of my own—looking for you." He came to stand within hugging distance of Nancy. "Looks like we found each other."

The nearness of him made Nancy forget all her problems. "I'm glad we did," she said. "I'm so glad, in fact, that I'm inviting you to go for a Coke. Right now."

"Sounds great to me."

"Good. I'll drive," Nancy said teasingly, "and let you see what my Mustang can do."

As they walked through the parking lot, Nancy spotted Jake Webb among the cars. Probably siphoning gas, she thought. Every time she saw him, she remembered how he'd threatened her on the stairs the day before. Was that his first threat? Or had he tried to scare her off before with the videotape?

Then Daryl put his hand casually on Nancy's shoulder and she forgot about Jake Webb and simply enjoyed the touch of Daryl Gray.

"How is it going, really?" Daryl asked again as they got into the Mustang. "Have you found any clues? Are any of the pieces fitting together yet?"

Nancy started the car with a roar. "I never thought I'd say this," she admitted with a wry smile, "but right now, the last thing on earth I want to do is solve a mystery."

Glad to be leaving, Nancy headed out of the parking lot and down Bedford Road. Daryl didn't ask any more questions about the case, and she was grateful. There'd be plenty of time to think about it later; just then, all she wanted to do was drive.

As they headed away from the high school, Bedford Road became narrow and winding. Through the trees Nancy caught glimpses of water.

"That's Bedford Lake," Daryl pointed out. "It has some nice secluded benches. Why don't you drive down there?"

Down is right, Nancy thought as the grade suddenly became steeper. She'd been doing about thirty-five and all of a sudden the needle climbed to fifty. A blind curve was coming up. Nancy put her foot on the brake. The pedal sank to the floor, and her stomach sank with it.

"Hey," Daryl said, "I don't want to sound like a driver's ed teacher, but don't you think you should slow down a little?"

Nancy couldn't answer him. The brakes were gone, and her car was shooting down the winding road, completely out of control!

Chapter

Six

THE CAR PICKED up speed, careening wildly down the hill. Nancy downshifted to second, then to first. The Mustang slowed, but not enough.

"Sharp curve coming up." Daryl spoke quietly, but Nancy heard the quiver in his voice. She couldn't blame him—she was too terrified to speak.

Hands glued to the wheel, Nancy guided the car into the curve, praying that she wouldn't meet another car coming up. The road remained clear, but it also grew steeper. And as she came out of the bend, she could see the stop sign at the bottom of the hill. It was still fifty yards away, but in her imagination she was already on top of it, could see the Mustang tearing into the intersection and colliding with whoever was unlucky enough to be in the wrong place at the wrong time.

Amazed that her hand was steady, Nancy reached over and slowly pulled up the hand-brake. It didn't work. The car was going so fast that the brakes had burned out.

The stop sign was looming up like a monster's claw in a 3-D movie. There was no time to think. Instinctively Nancy aimed her car at the soft shoulder on the opposite side of the road. With an impact that snapped their heads back, the Mustang hit the bank, went up on two wheels, and wobbled for what seemed like an eternity. But finally, with a bone-jarring thump, it landed upright.

Nancy shut her eyes and leaned her head on the steering wheel. She was breathing like a marathon runner. When she opened her eyes again, she saw Daryl pry his hand loose from the dashboard. "Well," he said with a gasp, "so that's what your Mustang can do."

Nancy reached for his hand and held on tight. She felt like crying, but when she opened her mouth, a giggle came out. It was a perfectly normal hysterical reaction, she told herself. Then she giggled again.

There was a smile in Daryl's voice as he said, "How about letting me in on the joke?"

"It's just"—Nancy tried to stop laughing and couldn't—"I remembered that my car is due for an inspection in two weeks. Now the gears are probably stripped, the front bumper has to be completely smashed, and the brakes are burned out—" This last thought brought Nancy out of her dreamworld.

Her car! What had gone wrong? True, it needed an inspection, but that was just an official thing. Besides, she'd had new brakes installed six weeks ago. Something awfully strange was going on, and whatever it was, Nancy had a definite feeling that it wasn't good. She pushed open the door and jumped out.

"Hey! Where're you going?" Daryl called, rolling down his window. He stuck his head out and saw Nancy kneeling by the left front wheel, peering underneath the fender. "What is it?" he asked.

Nancy stood up, so angry she could hardly see straight. "The brake cable," she said grimly. "It's been cut."

"What?! Are you sure? I don't get it. Who'd . . . ?"

"Wait!" Nancy held her hand up for quiet. Then she sniffed the air. Frowning, she ran to the back of the car and sniffed again.

"What's wrong now?!"

Nancy could hardly believe what she was going to say. "That rock we went over? I think it cracked the gas tank. Daryl, the car could blow! It could blow any second!" She started down the hill. "Get out of the car. Hurry up!"

There were no footsteps behind her. "Nancy!" she heard Daryl call. "Nancy, I can't open the door! It's jammed!"

Nancy didn't hesitate. She raced back to the car and fought with the door from the outside, but she couldn't get a good grip on the handle because the door was on an angle, leaning toward her.

She ran to the driver's side. The smell of gas fumes was stronger than ever.

"Get your seat belt off," she said to Daryl, finally managing to open her door. She helped him climb out. "Now let's *go!*" She grabbed his hand. "The car's already beginning to burn!" she said as they ran desperately down the hill.

When the car blew, they were only a few yards away from it. The force of the explosion flung them into the underbrush by the side of the road.

They clung to each other. For a moment, hardly able to speak, they stared at the burning sportscar.

"Nancy, are you all right?" Daryl whispered at last. His eyes were bright with concern.

Nancy nodded. Feeling the heat of Daryl's breath against her cheek, she hardly noticed her bruised knee and scratched arms. It seemed the most natural thing in the world for them to keep their arms around each other. Nancy closed her eyes and breathed deeply. When Daryl had first touched her two days before, in the hallway, she'd wondered what his arms would feel like. Now she knew—they felt fabulous.

But with that fabulous feeling came another feeling—guilt. It wasn't Ned whose arms were holding her; it wasn't Ned whose lips she was feeling, nor Ned whose voice was murmuring her name. And hadn't she said just three days before that nobody could compete with Ned Nickerson? Well, maybe no one could in the long run. But at the moment—in the short run—Daryl Gray was doing a pretty good job of it.

It was a dangerous moment, emotionally, and Nancy knew she wasn't ready to deal with it. Before Daryl's lips reached hers again, she eased herself gently from his arms.

"Hey," she said softly.

"Hey, yourself." Daryl's blue eyes were smiling. Looking at Nancy, he gave a long sigh. "So," he said in a throaty voice, "how about answering the question I never got a chance to ask. Who would do something crazy like this?"

"I have a pretty good idea." Anger made Nancy's voice tight. She pulled away and felt herself stiffen. "Does the name Jake Webb ring any bells?"

"Jake? Sure," Daryl said slowly, sitting up. "I can see him doing something like this. But there's no way you can prove it, is there?"

Nancy was silent for a moment. She was remembering Jake's threat on the stairs, remembering him in the parking lot half an hour ago, hearing that voice on the videotape: "Stick with shopping, Nancy Drew. It's a lot safer than snooping at Bedford High."

Well, she hadn't done much "snooping" yet, but she hadn't backed off either. Had Jake, for some reason, decided to stop her before she got any further?

"You're right," she said as she and Daryl got up and brushed the leaves and dirt off their clothes. "I can't prove it. But I think Jake's the one."

"So what are you going to do?"

"Talk to him about it," Nancy said. "First thing tomorrow morning."

"Hey, Nancy, I wouldn't do that," Daryl said quickly. "Jake Webb's not the kind of guy you go around accusing of something, believe me."

"I believe you," Nancy told him. "I also think he has some explaining to do."

Daryl took her hand, sounding really worried. "You shouldn't mess with that guy, Nancy!"

"I'm not going to mess with him, I'm just going to talk to him." In a way, Nancy was almost glad that Jake had given her something to think about. It took her mind off how she felt about Daryl, which was a mystery she didn't want to solve just then. "Please don't worry. I'll be careful," she said, flagging down a car that was passing slowly. "But Jake Webb is up to something, and I'm going to find out what it is."

"I think Daryl's right," George said as she drove toward Bedford High the next morning. Until Nancy got another car, George and Bess had to play chauffeur. "I think you should steer clear of this Jake Webb and go right to the police. Show them your car. Then let them deal with Jake."

"That's what I think, too." Bess leaned over the back seat and grinned at Nancy. "Now, tell us more about Daryl Gray."

"You'll probably meet him one of these days," Nancy said. She stared out at the beautiful Bedford houses, trying to decide the best way to approach Jake. Daryl was the least of her worries at the moment, even though she couldn't help remembering the kiss he'd given her after driving her home the previous night.

Before he'd kissed her, he'd tried once again to talk her out of confronting Jake. Nancy was touched that he was so worried about her, but she was sure she could handle Jake Webb. After all, she wasn't going to meet him in some dark alley; she was going to walk right up to him in the halls of Bedford High. She couldn't wait to see the look on his face when he saw that his gruesome plan hadn't worked—that she was alive and ready to take him on, the creep!

"What's happening?" George interrupted Nancy's thoughts, pointing to the wide front steps of the high school.

Nancy looked and saw at least half the student body milling around outside. The kids were talking in little clusters, waving their arms, pointing dramatically. Then she saw the police cars, one with its red lights still flashing.

"Well, at least you'll have police protection when you talk to Jake," Bess joked. "I wonder what they're here for?"

"Good question," Nancy said. Could Daryl have called them? She didn't think so. He'd tried to talk her out of dealing with Jake at least ten times, but he'd never once suggested that she go to the police, which was a little strange, when she thought about it.

She didn't think about it for long, though. As soon as she got out of the car, she joined the nearest group of kids.

"What happened?" she asked. "What's going on?"

One of the girls turned to her, fear and excitement in her eyes. "It's Jake Webb," she said breathlessly. "He's been killed!"

Chapter

Seven

NANCY WONDERED FOR a moment if she'd heard right. "Did you say killed—dead?"

"As a doornail!"

"But . . . how?"

"Nobody knows for sure," the girl went on, "but somebody found him about twenty minutes ago, and they say his neck's broken." She shivered. "It's awful, isn't it? I heard the guy who found him is still throwing up. Personally, I'm sure I would have passed out. I mean, can you imagine?"

Nancy could hardly imagine any of it. All night she'd been gearing up, getting ready to face Jake Webb, to accuse him, among other things, of trying to kill her. And in spite of what she'd told Daryl and Bess and George, she *had* been scared. Well, she wouldn't have to be scared anymore, not of Jake Webb.

Still finding the whole thing unbelievable, Nancy reported the news to Bess and George. Then she climbed the front steps and went into school. As she moved through the main hall, she heard bits and pieces of conversation that told her a little more about Jake Webb's demise:

"Right next to the video lab, at the bottom of the stairs—hard, cement stairs. Geez, no wonder the fall broke his neck."

"They say he's been dead for two hours—I wonder what he was doing here at six in the morning?"

"Probably planting a bomb."

"Too bad he fell first."

"Fell? The guy didn't fall, no way! Didn't you hear about his face?"

Jake's face. That's what Nancy heard most about on her walk through the hall. His face was bruised and cut. The bruises could have come from a fall down a flight of cement stairs. But not the cuts around his eyes, not his split lip.

Jake had been in a fight before he hit the hard floor in front of the lab. And if that was true, Nancy thought, then he didn't fall. He was pushed. And if he was pushed, then her investigation had just taken a giant leap—from vandalism to murder.

No one she heard even pretended to feel sorry that Jake was dead, and as she thought about Hunk, Hal, Connie, and who knew how many others, she realized that a lot of people around Bedford High would have wanted Jake to vanish. But who would have wanted it badly enough to give him that push?

When Nancy reached the scene of Jake's "accident," the police and the man from the coroner's office were still gathered there. The body, thank goodness, was gone, but the chalk outline remained.

She knew that if she talked to the police then and there, they'd listen to her. They'd probably even ask her to join their investigation.

But if she did that, she'd blow her cover. And if she did *that*, she might as well kiss the secrets of Bedford High good-bye.

Since the police were busy at the stairwell, Nancy decided that then might be a good time to check Jake Webb's locker. She wanted to look at the contents of that shoebox before anybody else got to it. What besides Connie's bracelet had Jake stashed away?

She was so busy wondering if Jake's locker would have any clues hidden in it, that she didn't see Daryl until she bumped into him.

"Daryl, hi!" Even with everything else on her mind, Nancy felt a warm rush of feeling at the sight of him. "I guess I don't need to ask if you've heard the news?"

"Hardly." Daryl took her hand, but he did it in an absentminded way. "I just talked to Mr. Parton," he said, his voice low enough that only Nancy could hear him. "He told me to tell you it's murder, definitely."

Nancy's eyes widened, but she wasn't really surprised. "Did Mr. Parton say anything about me, about what I should do?"

"Just that he wants you to stay on the case," Daryl whispered, "and to handle it your way."

"Great! I was hoping he'd say that." Nancy breathed a sigh of relief and squeezed Daryl's hand. "Now I can really follow some leads." She started to walk away but Daryl held her back.

"Wait a second," he said. "If Jake was the vandal, then your case is solved. You're into murder now, Nancy. I think you should back off."

"You've got to be kidding!" Nancy couldn't help feeling insulted. "Why should I back off? Do you think it's too complicated for me or something?"

"Hey, no, I didn't mean that." Daryl's violet eyes were full of worry. "It's just that it's probably going to get dangerous, Nancy. You don't have any idea what you're up against."

"No, I don't, but I'm going to find out." Nancy smiled at him. "Thanks for worrying

61

about me, but please try not to," she said. "Really. I can take care of myself." Out of the corner of her eye, she saw Carla Dalton heading toward them, and she couldn't resist planting a kiss on Daryl's cheek. She wanted to anyway, but having Carla as a witness made it even more fun. "Gotta go now," she told Daryl with a twinkle in her eye. "I'll talk to you later, let you know what I've found out."

The halls were still jammed with kids discussing the morning's main event, but luckily the final bell rang as Nancy reached Jake's locker. She was surprised that everyone was still marching to the sound of bells, on that day of all days, but it was a good thing old habits died hard. The hall cleared in a matter of minutes. Nancy pulled on a pair of rubber gloves—no sense leaving fingerprints for the police—and quickly broke into locker 515.

The shoebox was still there, but something else caught her eye first. With a grim smile, she pulled a pair of wire cutters off the shelf. Turning them over in her hands, Nancy thought how easily they must have snapped her brake cable.

Underneath the wire cutters was a small black box. Nancy recognized it immediately as a battery pack for a video camera. She would have bet her fifty-dollar designer jeans that Jake stole it from the video lab and used it to tape her and Bess and George on their shopping spree.

Finally Nancy took out the shoebox and lifted the lid, her heart beating with anticipation. Connie's bracelet was still there, along with a recent article from the school newspaper that carried a picture of Walt Hogan being brutally tackled during a game. The headline read, "The Hunk Gets Hit—He's Down But Not Out." The story went on to explain that if Walt missed the upcoming All-State Championship game because of injury, his badly needed football scholarship—and his ticket to the pros—might be in jeopardy. But Walt pooh-poohed the injury, claiming that nothing would stop him from playing in the All-State game.

At the bottom of the box, folded in half, was a wad of official-looking papers. As Nancy opened them she recognized them at once, without even reading the heading. They were SAT exams. There was just one difference between them and the ones she'd once toiled over—the set of exams in Jake's locker already had the answers marked in.

Nancy studied the curious contents of the box, trying to make sense out of them. She was positive now that Jake was the Bedford High vandal. The battery pack and the SATs pretty much proved that. But, looking at the bracelet, she wondered if he was also into stealing. It didn't really matter if he was, except for one

THE NANCY DREW FILES

thing—someone had killed him. And Nancy
was determined to find out why.

The police were going to be asking the same
questions, she knew, so she put the shoebox,
the wire cutters, and the battery pack back
where she'd found them. She closed the locker
door and was trying to come up with an excuse
for being late to her first class, when a voice
behind her said, "Well, if it isn't Nancy Drew,
girl detective. You always manage to be right in
the swing of the nastiest things."

Chapter

Eight

NANCY WHIRLED AROUND and came face to face with a tall, black-haired young woman whose vivid red lips were curled in a scornful smile.

Oh, great, Nancy thought. *This is exactly what I need—a snake in the grass like Brenda Carlton!*

As she looked at Brenda, standing there in her trendy trenchcoat, a notebook and pen in one hand, Nancy felt like laughing. Brenda had delusions of being an investigative reporter for *Today's Times,* her daddy's award-winning newspaper. But as far as Nancy was concerned, the only things Brenda did well were wear clothes—and mess up Nancy's investigations. She'd done that too many times for Nancy ever to trust her, and there she was again, smirking and lurking.

"Well, Brenda," Nancy said, "what are you doing here? Trying to play reporter?"

"I saw you first, girl wonder." Brenda gave Nancy a saccharine smile and flipped open her notebook. "Let's see," she said, pretending to scribble with her pen, "'When this reporter arrived at Bedford High, the first person she ran into was none other than Nancy Drew, *alleged* private detective.' How does that sound?"

If she talks any louder, Nancy thought, *the whole school'll know who I am.* "Okay, Brenda, what do you *think* I'm doing here? What do sleuths usually do at the scene of the crime?"

"Scene of the crime? This looks like a high-school locker to me, not the bottom of a stairwell." Brenda's green eyes swept over Nancy in a quick, but all-seeing, glance. Pointing a red-nailed finger at Nancy's history book, she smiled. "Oh, I see! You're posing as a student. How clever of you! I'm surprised you thought of it."

Dropping the sweet voice, Brenda went on, "Now, why don't you give me a few more details about what's going on here? If you don't, all your little high school friends are going to find out real fast what you're really up to. And I have a feeling you wouldn't like that at all."

"Is that a threat, Brenda?"

"Of course it is, Nancy. So how about it? Are you going to give me the whole story?"

Nancy sighed. What choice did she have? The case was complicated and dangerous; she couldn't solve it and battle Brenda Carlton at the same time. "All right," she said, gritting her teeth, "I'll make a deal with you."

"A deal?" Brenda's silky eyebrows drew together in a frown. "What kind of deal?"

"The kind of deal that'll give you the exclusive story," Nancy told her. "Face it, Brenda, the police aren't going to give you the time of day. And right now, I know more about what's going on than they do. So when it's over, I'll be able to give you a really sensational story, right down to the last juicy detail."

Nancy watched Brenda's frown change to a smile. Probably seeing her byline already, she thought. "There's just one catch," she warned. "I give you the story *after* I've solved the case, not before. If you want to know everything I do, stay out of my way and keep your mouth shut about who I am. Think you can manage that?"

For about thirty seconds Brenda wavered between taking her chances with the police then, or making a deal with Nancy for later. Finally she reached a decision. "Well, all right," she said, pouting. "I'll do it your way. But," she warned, "you'd better keep your part of the bargain or the only role you'll ever play again is 'unemployed detective.'"

Nancy bit her lip to keep back any insulting remarks that might blow the deal. But as she watched Brenda stroll away, she promised herself that someday, she was going to close that reporter's notebook for good.

With the police swarming all over the school, Nancy's investigation didn't get very far. All the kids were talking about Jake, of course, but even so, Nancy wasn't able to learn much. All the kids had opinions, but they were just gossip and speculation. Nancy wanted to talk to the three people whom she knew had some connection with Jake—Walt Hogan, Hal Morgan, and Connie Watson. She didn't see Walt at all, and Hal didn't hear her call to him after American history, or maybe he didn't want to hear her. He looked extremely nervous. So did Connie, who once more acted as if Nancy had developed a sudden case of overwhelmingly bad breath.

If anyone has any answers, Nancy thought, *they're not admitting it.* Nancy didn't have any answers either, but she thought she might find something in the video lab. Obviously, Jake had been "borrowing" the school's video equipment; maybe Nancy could find some clue in the lab that would tell her why.

The door was locked again, so Nancy used her credit card. As she worked the lock, she thought she heard a noise coming from inside the lab. She stopped, listening. There it was, a faint thump, as if someone had dropped something on the floor.

Could a policeman be in there? It was four o'clock in the afternoon; the halls were empty of students, and Nancy had watched the two patrol cars drive off half an hour ago. Still, they might have left one officer behind to guard the school. If they had, Nancy decided that it wouldn't help her case any to get caught.

She raised her hand and knocked loudly on the door. Then she listened again. No sound this time. After a few more loud raps, she decided that whatever she'd heard hadn't come from inside. The empty halls picked up sounds from everywhere. The noise could have come from the floor above. She worked the lock again and pushed open the door.

The room was a wreck. Cables and wires were strewn across the floor like uncoiled snakes, and at least half the tapes had been pulled from the shelves and lay in scattered piles on the desk and the floor. Nancy knew the police must have searched the place after finding that battery pack in Jake's locker. Either that (and they were real slobs), or somebody else had been there. Could that someone have been Jake's murderer, after some kind of evidence?

Suddenly Nancy didn't like all the silence around her. She cleared her throat noisily and told herself that if the murderer had been there, he (or she) was probably long gone. And from the look of things, he hadn't found what he was after. Maybe she could beat him to it, she thought.

Quietly Nancy closed the door behind her and stepped over several lengths of cable to the middle of the room. Her gaze fell on a neat row of about thirty tapes, still on the shelf.

Nancy crossed the room to the shelf and saw that the tapes were just rock videos. Glancing at the familiar names, Nancy thought maybe they weren't worth her attention. But then, one of the labels caught her eye. Right next to "Material Girl" (which made her think immediately of Brenda Carlton) was a tape labeled "I Spy."

"I Spy"? It wasn't any rock group Nancy had heard of. Maybe I Spy was a Bedford High group. Nancy decided to have a quick look at it. She just hoped the music was good.

After the first few seconds Nancy wished there *were* music. The tape was completely silent, but the images were so unbelievable that music would have made it seem like a joke, or some kind of fantasy. Instead, Nancy knew she was seeing reality.

The first person on the tape was Hunk Hogan. He was sitting on a bench in what must have been the locker room. No one else was visible, and when Walt glanced cautiously around, Nancy decided that *he* had decided he was alone.

After another careful look, the star tackle reached into the duffel bag at his feet and took out a roll of white tape. Obviously in great pain, he began to wrap it around his rib cage, wincing the whole time. Nancy remembered the article in Jake's locker that told of Walt betting all his hopes for a football scholarship on the upcoming All-State game. From the look of him, he'd be lucky to get dressed for that game, much less play in it. Walt was hurt, but he'd hidden it—from everyone except Jake Webb.

The video lab was stuffy and hot, but Nancy shivered as a chill ran up her spine. She'd been right—this case was much, much bigger than anyone thought. And the "I Spy" tape was an extremely hot piece of evidence. Too hot to be watching smack in the middle of Bedford High.

Quickly Nancy pushed the stop button and ejected the tape. She was reaching for the monitor to shut it off when she heard a noise. Or thought she did. She snapped off the monitor and listened. For a few seconds the only sound she heard was the blood pulsing in her ears. But then came another noise, a squeak, as if someone had stopped leaning on a table. Or a door!

At the far end of the room was a door marked "Supplies," and as Nancy listened again, she heard another muffled sound. Someone was in that supply room. And it wasn't a policeman. A policeman would have been out by then, asking her what she was doing there, demanding that she turn over the tape, which was crucial evidence in a murder investigation. And who else would be interested in such crucial evidence but Jake's killer?

For an instant Nancy froze. If the killer was in that supply closet, Nancy's life was in danger. So was the evidence. She knew she had to get out fast. Noiselessly she dropped the videotape into her bag. She wanted to run, but she was afraid of alerting whoever was behind the door. Slowly, quietly, she inched her way across the lab to the hall door. With a sweaty hand, she eased it open and slipped out. Then she tore down the hall as fast as she could.

It was late afternoon and the hall was dark. The stairs leading to the first floor were even darker, but Nancy didn't slow down. She jumped the last four steps, skidded around a corner, and raced toward the main door. As she neared it she thought she heard footsteps on the stairs, but she didn't bother to turn around and make sure. Still moving fast, she rammed into the panic bar, expecting the door to fly open.

The door didn't budge! Nancy was certain she heard footsteps behind her. She gave the door another desperate push. Nothing.

Okay, she thought. I guess it's showdown time. Taking a deep breath, Nancy turned around, ready to face the intruder.

Chapter

Nine

Nancy closed her eyes, waited a beat, then forced them open. The dark hall loomed ahead of her. She focused on the bottom of the staircase, held her breath, and waited again. All she saw were shadows, and all she heard was her own heartbeat. No one was there. Not now, anyway.

Letting out her breath in a sigh of relief, Nancy leaned against the door—and found herself falling backward as the door opened easily, depositing her on her rear on the stone steps outside.

Of course, she thought, picking herself up,

it's a double door. You just pushed the wrong side.

Glad to be outdoors, Nancy took several deep gulps of the cool autumn air. Then she saw George's car make a slow turn around the side of the building.

"Hey!" Nancy waved her hand and ran down the front steps. "Here I am!"

The car slowed, and Bess stuck her head out the window. "We were just about to give up and go home," she said. "George has been driving around this parking lot forever, but I kept telling her you probably got a ride with Daryl."

"I wish I *had* been with Daryl," Nancy said as she climbed into the back seat. "He's a lot more fun. And a lot safer, too."

"Why? What happened?" George wanted to know.

As they drove away from Bedford High, Nancy filled them in on everything that had happened, from the details of Jake's murder to her own scary escape from the video lab. "And wait'll you see the tape," she said, patting her duffel bag. "It'll never win an Oscar, but it's one of the most fascinating movies I've ever seen."

When they got back to Nancy's River Heights home and settled down to watch, they soon discovered that the tape was even more fascinating than Nancy had predicted. And Walt

Hogan wasn't the only person Jake had made into a star.

Bess sighed as she watched Hunk tape his ribs. "How can he stand to play when he's in pain?"

"It's his only chance for that scholarship," George said. "If he doesn't get that, he'll never make the pros."

"Yeah, and he wasn't about to let anything stand in his way," Nancy commented. "Not the pain, and not Jake."

"Poor guy." Bess sighed again. "At least Jake Webb can't bother him anymore. Do you suppose Hunk is glad, deep down, that Jake's dead?"

"He wouldn't be human if he weren't," Nancy said. "But I have a question for you. Do you suppose Walt Hogan had anything to do with getting rid of Jake?"

Before either of her friends had a chance to answer that startling question, another face appeared on the television screen—the smooth, round face of Connie Watson.

"Who's that?" Bess asked.

"A girl from Bedford High," Nancy told her, and scooted to the edge of the couch, wondering what on earth shy Connie could possibly have done to get a part in Jake Webb's "movie."

She soon found out. The "setting" was a

sidewalk sale in fashionably quaint downtown Bedford. All the shopowners had brought their wares out to the sidewalks on what looked like a sunny autumn day. Crowds of shoppers strolled by, eating ice cream cones and stopping to look at paintings, handmade pottery, and furniture, and, Nancy noticed with a sense of dread, jewelry.

Nancy knew what was coming the minute she saw the jewelry display. Sure enough, the camera panned the crowd and focused on Connie Watson, a large shopping bag in her hand.

Nancy's heart sank as she watched what happened next. Connie picked up a bracelet—the one Nancy had seen her wearing—and admired it for a minute. Then she seemed to ask the shopowner the price and reluctantly put it back on the display table.

"Now just watch," Nancy told her friends. "She's about to make the biggest mistake of her life."

Hovering at the edge of the jewelry table, Connie waited until the owner was busy with about six customers at once. Then a close-up, courtesy of Jake the cameraman, showed her hook a finger under the bracelet and slide it into her conveniently waiting shopping bag. The camera pulled back then, and Connie melted into the crowds that filled the sidewalk.

But Jake wasn't through with Connie. His

next shot caught her going up the front steps of the high school, the early morning sun glinting on her new gold bracelet.

"So far we've seen somebody covering up an injury and somebody shoplifting," George said. "I wonder what's next?"

"I'm not sure I want to know," Bess shuddered. "This whole thing gives me the creeps."

"Oh, no!" Nancy pointed to the television screen and shook her head in amazement. "It's Hal Morgan. I should have guessed."

The next installment of Jake's horror show followed Hal, nervous nail-chewer and future Harvard scholar, straight to the door of the office of Bedford High's principal. Like Walt Hogan, Hal probably thought he was alone, because he glanced furtively around before entering the office.

The camera didn't follow him inside. It held steady on the closed door. Five seconds passed and then the door opened. Out came Hal, who stood still, obviously trying to work something out in his mind.

"You can almost hear the wheels turning," George remarked. "He's empty-handed. I wonder what he's after."

"Answers," Nancy said.

Bess looked confused. "Huh?"

"Just keep watching," Nancy told her. "You'll see what I mean."

Having worked out the problem, Hal walked

quickly to another door. Without bothering to look behind him, he opened it and went inside. The camera stayed on the sign on the door, which read, "Counselors' Offices."

When Hal came out this time, he wasn't empty-handed. He didn't look worried or confused anymore, either. The camera gave Nancy and her two friends a brief glimpse of Hal's triumphant smile, but it lingered longest on what he held in his hands—answer books for the Scholastic Aptitude Tests.

"How could Jake tape that without Hal seeing him?" George asked.

"He really knew his video stuff," Nancy said. "He probably set that one up by remote control. That would explain why the offices had been broken into earlier. He must have been rigging up the camera." She thought a minute. "I wouldn't even be surprised if he gave Hal the idea for stealing those answers, just so he could tape the whole thing. After all, Jake did work in the principal's office."

Wavering black bars and dancing snowflakes had appeared on the screen, and Nancy turned off the VCR and the television. "I'm glad that's over," she commented.

"So am I." Bess stood up and stretched. "I don't know why, but movies always make me hungry, even this one. Let's go see what's in the refrigerator."

In the refrigerator they found leftover takeout Chinese food. Sitting at the round oak kitchen table, the three friends discussed Jake's tape between bites of lo mein and shrimp fried rice.

"Obviously, Connie didn't buy that bracelet," Nancy said. "She stole it. And after Hal lost so much ground trying to become class president, he knew the only way he'd get into Harvard was to cheat on the SAT so that he could get unusually high scores."

Bess poured herself some more diet soda. "And poor Hunk. It must be awful to feel so desperate!"

"Why do you think Jake did it?" George asked. "Money?"

"Maybe." Nancy crunched thoughtfully on an ice cube. "But I think it was more of a power trip. He would find someone's weak spot and dig in. Jake liked knowing everybody's secrets. That's probably how he found out about me in time to tape us at the mall that day. He must have had his ear to Mr. Parton's door when Mr. Parton talked to my father. He knew my 'secret,' too. He liked being king of the mountain."

"Yeah, well somebody finally pushed him off," Bess said. "And no wonder. He must have had things on half the kids in school."

"But he only has three people on tape," George pointed out. "Nancy, do you really think one of them killed him?"

Nancy shrugged her shoulders in frustration.

Later, after George and Bess had left, she took a long hot shower, trying to come up with an answer to George's question.

Walt Hogan was strong enough to give Jake that final push, she thought, especially if he'd been angry. And Hal wasn't exactly a lightweight. If he'd been desperate enough, he might just have decided to challenge Jake.

She couldn't rule out Connie either. Sweet, gossipy Connie Watson was as strong a candidate for murderer as the two guys. Anyone could have pushed him.

Nancy turned around and let the warm, misty spray roll off her back. Jake Webb wasn't just a thief and a vandal, she thought, he was the Bedford High Blackmailer. Getting power from kids who'd made mistakes must have given him a kick, a sick, sadistic kick.

But somebody had finally kicked him back. The question was, who? Was it really one of the kids on the tape—Walt or Connie or Hal? Could one of those three Bedford High students have been so determined to get out from under Jake's thumb that he or she murdered him to keep a secret safe?

Chapter

Ten

Nancy pushed her sloppy joe aside and reached for Daryl's hand across the cafeteria table. "I need a favor."

"Just ask," Daryl said with a smile. "What? You need a ride home after school?"

"Not exactly," Nancy answered, looking mysterious. "I lucked out. This morning my dad surprised me with a new Mustang GT Convertible."

Daryl rolled his eyes. "You've got to be kidding."

"The deal is I'll pay him back when the insurance money comes through." Nancy grinned sheepishly. "Plus twenty years allow-ance, I've been told."

"Poor baby," Daryl teased her, leaning close enough to brush his lips against her ear. "So what's the favor? You want me to test-drive your new toy?"

Nancy didn't tease back. "No," she said, forcing herself to pull back from Daryl's hand-some face. "I want to tell you something, but you have to promise not to breathe a word of it to anyone."

"I can keep a secret, Detective. Promise."

They were alone at a table in the farthest corner of the cafeteria. Any of the kids who happened to glance their way probably thought they were having a private lovers' talk. But love was the farthest thing from Nancy's mind at that moment as she quietly told Daryl about Jake Webb's blackmail videotape.

When she finished, she sat back and sipped her iced tea, waiting for Daryl's reaction.

But Daryl must have been so stunned he couldn't think of anything to say. He just stared at her with wide, dark-blue eyes, his face almost blank.

"It's okay to be shocked," Nancy said. "I was, and I'm the detective."

"Yeah, I . . ." Daryl shook his head and whistled softly. "Wow. I *am* shocked. I mean, it's unbelievable."

"It is—unless you've seen the tape."

"So what are you going to do with it?" Daryl asked. "Turn it over to the police?"

Nancy shook her head. "I guess I'll have to give it to them pretty soon. But since Mr. Parton is letting me handle this my way, I'd like to work on my own just a little longer. For now, that tape's going to stay safe at home, where I can keep an eye on it."

Daryl nodded. "I guess you think one of those kids killed Jake, huh?"

"I don't know what I think yet," Nancy admitted. "I don't want to believe it at all."

"But they're the only ones on the tape, isn't that what you said?" Daryl asked quickly.

"Yes, but somehow I just . . ." Nancy sighed.

"Jake really blew it for everybody, didn't he?" Daryl looked sympathetic and concerned, just the way Ned would have reacted, Nancy thought. Then Daryl leaned across the table and gave her one of his sexiest looks. "Don't take this wrong, Detective, but be careful, okay?"

Warmed by Daryl's concern and support, not to mention his touch, Nancy spent the rest of the afternoon—in between classes—tracking down the three "stars" of Jake's videotape.

She found Hal in the library, just beginning a

paper that she happened to know was due in two days. "Hi," she whispered as she joined him at the study table. "I thought you'd be finished with that by now. Everybody says you're a real whiz."

Hal gave her a nervous smile and shrugged. "Even whizzes get behind sometimes."

"Well, I guess you don't have to worry, though," Nancy went on. "I mean, if you're smart enough to get into Harvard and write papers for Jake Webb on the side, then—"

That got Hal's attention. "What do you mean?" he interrupted in a whisper. "I don't know what you're talking about."

"Really?" Nancy was all innocence. "Gee, I was sure I heard you and Jake talking about it in the hall, right after that pop quiz, remember?"

"No. You didn't. I mean, you must have heard wrong." Hal stood up, gathering his stuff together with shaky hands. "Look, I've got to get going."

"Oh, too bad," Nancy said. "I was going to ask your advice. See, I'll be taking the SATs soon and I thought maybe you could give me some hints on how to handle them. Everybody says your scores were sky-high. How did you do it? Or is that a secret?"

Hal looked so nervous, Nancy thought he might break down right there in the library. But he managed to hold himself together long enough to mumble something about "luck." Then he rushed out of the room, but not before shooting Nancy a look of pure terror.

Nancy wasn't sure what to make of it. Was Hal scared because of the SATs he'd stolen, or had he done something much worse than stealing and cheating? She decided to try again with him, but first she wanted to talk to the other two.

Walt Hogan wasn't hard to find. He stood out like a redwood in a grove of saplings, and she spotted him right before fifth period, heading out one of the side doors. *Good*, she said to herself. *You were looking for an excuse to cut calculus anyway*.

Nancy followed Walt across the campus toward the track, where she watched him run two laps before he stopped, throwing himself down on the grass. He was gasping as if he'd just run a three-minute mile, and she figured he must still be in pain.

"Tired?" Nancy asked pleasantly as she dropped into the grass beside him.

"Yeah." Walt grunted a couple of times and then opened his eyes. "Do I know you?"

"Well, we met," Nancy said. "Monday, remember? We sort of bumped into each other in the hall and Daryl Gray introduced us. I'm Nancy Drew."

"Yeah, sure." Walt didn't look sure at all. "How's it going?"

"Fine." Nancy plucked some grass and twisted it around her finger. "I watched you at practice the other day," she said. "You really amaze me. I mean, I fell off the trampoline and I could barely walk, so I know what you're going through."

"What do you mean, what I'm going through?" Walt asked.

"The pain," Nancy said. "Jake Webb told me all about—"

"Webb?" Walt broke in. "What kind of business did you have with that scum?"

"No business," Nancy said quickly. "He just explained about your injury and I wanted you to know that I understand."

"Look!" Walt jumped to his feet and stood towering over her. "I don't know what that slime told you, but whatever it was, he was lying!"

Nancy got to her feet and faced him. "Hey, okay," she said. "Don't get excited. I just thought—"

"Don't think!" Walt shouted. He took a step toward Nancy, and for a second she thought he was going to hit her. "Just get out of my sight! There's no pain because there's no injury, you understand?"

With an angry glare, Walt turned and slowly

walked toward the school. Nancy let her breath out. She'd taken a few judo classes, but not nearly enough to prepare her to face a raging, 200-pound football player.

Walt was touchy, to put it mildly, but Nancy still didn't have anything more than suspicions to go on. *No more hinting,* she told herself. *With Connie, just come right out and say what's on your mind. As horrible as the truth is, you have to confront her with it. At least you won't have to worry about being attacked. You hope.*

Chapter

Eleven

NANCY FOUND CONNIE Watson in the gym after school, watching cheerleader practice. She climbed the bleachers to her side.

"I have to talk to you," she said quietly. "About Jake Webb. And your bracelet. And a videotape I found."

Connie's round face flushed and then drained of color until it resembled a full moon. "I . . . I don't . . ." she stammered.

"Look," Nancy went on, ignoring the girl's panicked eyes, "the police found your bracelet in Jake's locker. And I know it's yours because I saw the videotape—the one Jake made of you stealing it. I haven't shown it to the police yet. But I will unless you tell me everything you know about how Jake was murdered."

Tears ran down Connie's cheeks, making them glisten under the bright gym lights. "It all started at the beginning of the school year. See, that bracelet wasn't the only thing I stole," she admitted. "I took a sweater the first time, and it was so easy I decided to try for a jacket." Connie swallowed hard. "Only that time I got caught. It's all in my school file."

"And since Jake worked in the office, he found out about it," Nancy commented.

Connie nodded and took a shaky breath. "I didn't know he knew, of course. But then, after I took the bracelet . . . Well, I know it was wrong but I wanted it so much, and there was no way I could afford it! I promised myself it was the last time. But then . . ."

She wiped her face and sniffed loudly. ". . . Then Jake came strutting along, said he had a 'movie' he wanted me to see. I nearly died when I saw it! I told him I was going to return the bracelet, but that slug made me wear it. When I tried to get rid of it, he stopped me and kept it himself. He said he knew all about my shoplifting record and that if he told anyone about the bracelet, I'd probably go to jail. And he was right!

"So after that, I had to do everything he asked." Connie shuddered. "Everything. I hoped that when he died, my secret would die with him."

Nancy felt terrible, but she had to keep pushing or she'd never get to the bottom of the mystery. "But Jake didn't just die," she said. "Someone killed him."

"I know, I know," Connie moaned. Then she looked at Nancy sharply. "I didn't do it! I'm not sorry he's dead, but I didn't kill him—and I can't believe you think I might have!"

With a sob, Connie ran down the bleacher steps and out of the gym. Nancy felt helpless. She wished she could have told Connie everything would be okay. But Connie had as much reason to knock off Jake as anyone else he'd blackmailed. Until Nancy found out who did it, she couldn't afford to feel sorry for anybody, not even sweet Connie Watson.

Still thinking about the answers she didn't have, Nancy left the gym and walked outside to her car. Daryl Gray was leaning against the driver's door, and Nancy's stomach did a little flip at the sight of him.

"I can tell by the look on your face that your 'interviews' didn't go too well," he said when she reached his side.

"You're right," Nancy admitted. "I'm not much further along than I was last night. But I'll figure it out eventually." She looked at him with a mock frown. "What are you doing here, anyway? I didn't think you'd ever come within fifty feet of a car of mine."

"When you want to be with somebody enough, you have to take chances." Daryl put a hand on Nancy's shoulder and brought his lips close to her ear. "Besides," he whispered, "I have an ulterior motive." He pulled open the door for her. "What I really want, aside from spending some time with you, is to see that tape."

"You mean 'The Secrets of Bedford High?'"

"Yeah. It sounds wild." Daryl shut the door after her and leaned down, his head in the window. "No, really, I thought maybe I could help. I know all those people better than you do. Maybe I can find some clues."

"It sounds good to me," Nancy said. "Let's go."

"You lead, I'll follow," Daryl said, and walked off toward his Porsche.

Half an hour later, the two of them were in Nancy's house, sitting close together on the beige couch in the den, sipping Cokes and looking at the Jake Webb production.

Daryl watched carefully but didn't say much, and Nancy was acutely aware of his closeness in the darkened room. As Connie Watson faded into the crowds of shoppers, Daryl brought his arm up and around Nancy's shoulder, his hand resting lightly on the back of her neck.

By the time Connie was walking up the

school steps, neither Daryl nor Nancy was watching. Their eyes were on each other.

"I hate to tell you this," Daryl said softly, "but I didn't see anything that might help you out."

"That's okay," Nancy whispered. "I'm glad you came over anyway."

As if they'd both thought of it at the same time, they moved their heads closer together until their lips were touching. Nancy slid her hands up Daryl's arms, felt his thick blond hair under her fingers, felt his lips press against hers. She could hear her heart pounding in her ears, and then suddenly she heard another sound—the doorbell.

Reluctant, but almost relieved, Nancy disentangled herself from Daryl's arms and stood up. "Bad timing, huh?"

"The worst," Daryl groaned ruefully.

The doorbell chimed again and Nancy went down the hall to answer it.

"Nan, hi!" Bess's smile changed to a gape as she stared at Nancy. "Were you taking a nap or something?"

"No, why?"

"You look a little . . . wrinkled," George pointed out.

"No, I was just—" Nancy stopped when she realized that her friends were staring at something behind her. Turning, she saw Daryl walking down the hall toward them, smoothing his hair with one hand and straightening his shirt with the other.

After a quick introduction Daryl turned to Nancy. "I think I'd better get going," he said with a warm smile. "See you tomorrow, okay?"

Bess could hardly wait until he was out the door. "Wow," she said breathily. "No wonder you look so glassy-eyed, Nancy. He's gorgeous!"

"For once I can't argue," George said.

"If I hadn't just met somebody else," Bess went on, "—and by the way, his name's Alan Wales, Nancy, wait'll you see him—I'd definitely fall in love with Daryl Gray. What were you two up to, anyway?"

Nancy was saved from explaining by another bell—the telephone. "Nancy," Hannah called from the kitchen. "It's for you. It's Ned."

"Thanks, Hannah," Nancy called back. "I'll take it in my bedroom." With a flustered smile, she turned to Bess and George. "I'll meet you in the den in a couple of minutes. Oh, turn off the tape machine, would you? I forgot."

"I can't imagine why," Bess teased.

Alone in her room Nancy tried to compose herself before she picked up the extension. Would Ned hear anything in her voice that would reveal what she'd just done? She hoped not. After all, Daryl was exciting, but Ned Nickerson was the one she loved. Wasn't he?

"Ned?"

"Hey, Nancy. How're you doing? I miss you."

She could hear the smile in his voice. "I miss you, too," she told him. "How's life at the university?"

"Busy. I've got good news, but first, tell me how the case is going."

"Well, I'll put it this way—it's still going." Nancy didn't really want to get into it. She might have to mention Daryl and she wasn't ready for that. "What's your good news?"

"I'm coming down this weekend."

"To River Heights?"

"Where else? That's where *you* are, isn't it?" Ned laughed. "What's the matter, don't you want to see me?"

"Are you kidding? Of course I do!" Nancy could say that truthfully, but still, she wondered what the weekend would be like. After all, she had a date with Daryl for the dance. What would Ned think about that? "When will you get here?" she asked.

"Tomorrow, early afternoon sometime. I'll call you as soon as I get there. Nancy?" Ned lowered his voice. "I can't wait to see you. Let's do something special."

"You're on," Nancy said with a grin, although she couldn't imagine what they'd do, not if she was busy with Daryl.

After she hung up, she tried to figure out whether to tell Ned everything about the case, including her two "close encounters" with Daryl, or to keep those incidents a secret and just pass Daryl off as one of her contacts in the case.

She was staring at the phone and chewing on a fingernail when George stuck her head around the door. "Nancy? Could you come in the den? There's something you should see."

Glad to be distracted, Nancy followed George down the hall and into the den. "Bess was just about to turn the VCR off when something came on," George explained. "I guess Jake had one more scene and he put it at the very end of the tape."

"Who is it?" Nancy asked. "What other poor slob did Jake have in the wringer?"

"Oh, Nancy, it's not just another poor slob," Bess said. "Look."

George pushed the play button and a face appeared on the television screen. Nancy didn't say a word. She couldn't. The face belonged to Daryl Gray!

Chapter

Twelve

IN DISBELIEVING SILENCE Nancy watched her "contact" in front of an unseen video camera. She had to keep reminding herself that it wasn't a performance. It was for real.

Scene One—Daryl got into his Porsche and drove off, the camera lingering on a sign for Route 110 East.

Scene Two—The Porsche pulled into the parking lot of a tacky-looking diner called the Red Caboose. Daryl got out of the car, walked across the street, and stood waiting on the sidewalk. Jake had obviously stayed behind, hidden somewhere in the Red Caboose lot.

Scene Three—A heavyset man with thick hair and a bushy mustache joined Daryl on the sidewalk. Jake zoomed in for a closer shot. The camera zeroed in on an identification tag clipped to the man's pocket. Nancy tried desperately to read the name. She thought she could make out an *M* and a *D,* but she wasn't sure. Jake hadn't been able to get a tight enough shot. Daryl and the man exchanged a few words, and then the man handed Daryl a small envelope, which Daryl stuffed in his jeans pocket. The man walked away, revealing on the chain-link fence behind him a sign, about one foot square. The letters were unreadable.

Scene Four—Another shot of Daryl in his car, this time passing the high school on Bedford Road.

Scene Five—The Porsche turned into a drive. No house was visible from the road, just an intricately scrolled wrought-iron fence on each side of the drive.

That was it. Five short scenes that blew Nancy's world apart. Less than an hour earlier, she'd been in Daryl's arms, a victim of his warm eyes and smooth personality. Then suddenly she'd discovered that he, too, was a victim of Jake Webb's scheming mind.

A few things began to make sense—the way Daryl had tried to talk her out of dealing with Jake, his eagerness to know how the case was going and to see the tape. With a shudder,

Nancy wondered what would have happened if he'd stayed long enough to see himself on the screen. Would he have killed Nancy for the tape, the way he might—just might—have killed Jake?

Pushing that awful thought from her mind, Nancy jumped up and turned the tape off. Then she started pacing around the room.

"Nancy," Bess asked, "are you okay?"

"Just totally confused." Nancy managed a laugh. "I mean, obviously Jake had something on Daryl. But what? The tape really doesn't show him doing anything wrong."

"It doesn't show much of anything," Bess agreed. "He just went someplace, met a man, and then went someplace else. I know!" she said. "Maybe he had a gambling thing going. You know, running numbers."

That made sense, Nancy thought. After all, with his father practically bankrupt, Daryl would want to keep up his slick lifestyle somehow. Gambling wasn't so terrible, she told herself hopefully.

"Well, we're not getting anywhere sitting around talking about it," George pointed out.

"You're right. Let's get going. I want to try to follow Daryl's route on the tape." Nancy grabbed the keys to her car. "We know what the others did. Now let's find out what Daryl's secret is."

Nancy's new car sped along Route 110. "Just

keep your eyes open for that diner," she reminded her friends.

"I won't miss it," Bess said. "I'm famished."

"We're not going there to eat," George told her.

"I know, but it wouldn't hurt to get a takeout order. I was so busy with Alan that I didn't even get lunch. Oh, Nancy," Bess went on, "I can't wait for you to meet Alan! He's not only good-looking, he's talented."

"At what?"

"He plays the guitar, and he's really serious about it. I'm sure he'll be a superstar someday," Bess said loyally. "Oh, I just remembered! His group's playing for the Bedford High dance tomorrow night!"

"Hey!" cried George. "Look on your right! It's the Red Caboose."

Just as Daryl had done, Nancy pulled into the parking lot, and the three girls got out. Facing away from the diner, across Route 110, they could see the chain-link fence, and now that they had a full view, they could see several of the small, square signs attached to the fence at regular intervals.

Beyond the fence was a vast complex of buildings. As Nancy and her friends crossed the street to the sidewalk where Daryl had met the man, Nancy wondered if the buildings were a factory of some kind.

Bess reached the fence first. "'Private—

Authorized Personnel Only,' " she read from one of the signs. Then she was quiet as Nancy and George joined her and read what was printed below that, in smaller letters. "U.S. Government."

"I didn't know there were any government offices out here," George said. "What is it, I wonder. A research place or something?"

"Let's find out," Nancy said. "I'm sure anybody who works at the Red Caboose knows what it is." She spoke calmly, but inside she was becoming very nervous. What could Daryl possibly have to do with the U.S. Government?

"It's an Air Force defense plant, honey," the man behind the counter said, in answer to Nancy's question. "They're up to their ears in secrets over there—designs for bombs, blueprints for nifty little radar devices that'll track down a missile before it's even left the ground, stuff like that." He gave the counter a swipe with his dishcloth and shook his head. "Tell you the truth, I get scared sometimes. If the United States is ever attacked, you can bet some country's got a bomb picked out for that place. And you know what that means for the Red Caboose."

Nancy and George were reeling from the idea that Daryl might be involved in spying somehow. Bess tried to perk them up as they walked out to the car. "Look," she said hopefully, "it might not be as bad as it seems. We don't know what that man on the tape gave Daryl. Maybe Daryl started a private messenger service."

"Maybe," Nancy said. But her thoughts were whirling around madly. Jake wouldn't have bothered with Daryl if Daryl were innocent. But what exactly was he guilty of? And how big was this case going to get? It had started out as petty vandalism, then it moved up to blackmail, and then to murder. Now what? Could it really be espionage? "Let's take a ride to Bedford," she said. "I want to find out exactly where Daryl delivered that envelope. That must be what he did, even though Jake didn't get it on tape."

It was dark by the time they reached Bedford Road, and as they drove by the high school, the road became darker. This was the super-rich section of Bedford, "The Mansion Mile," as Nancy had heard someone in school call it. But from the road, with high shrubbery and thick groves of trees masking the grounds, it was hard to see any landmarks.

Finally, though, George spotted the wrought-iron fence they'd seen on the tape, and Nancy turned into what seemed like a private drive. There was no gate and no sign to tell them whose property they were on.

"What do we do now?" Bess asked. "Pretend we're lost?"

"Good idea." Nancy drove through the opening in the fence.

As soon as they were on the property, the drive curved sharply to reveal a gate anchored to two moss-covered pillars. In the glare of the headlights the girls could easily read the sign posted on the gate: "U.S.S.R.—Private Property."

"U.S.S.R.?" Bess said. "What country are we in, anyway?"

"I think it's an estate, a kind of compound for diplomats," George told them. "I remember reading that a lot of countries buy foreign property so their officials can have someplace to go to relax. We're not all that far from the U.N., you know."

"We're not all that far from the defense plant, either," Nancy said.

Before anyone had a chance to comment on that remark, the gate swung open and searchlights flooded the area. The girls heard the sound of an engine and saw a pair of headlights round a curve in the drive in front of them. The headlights were getting closer fast, and they were heading straight for Nancy's car!

Chapter

Thirteen

THE FLOODLIGHTS LIT up the Mustang, throwing everything outside it into pitch darkness, except for the two headlights. They were dancing over the bumpy drive, looming closer and closer.

"Who do you suppose that is?" Bess squinted in the glare. "It's coming awfully fast!"

George cleared her throat. "Somehow, I don't think it's a welcoming committee."

"Let's get out of here!" cried Nancy.

As the headlights approached the gate, Nancy stepped on the gas, steered the Mustang into a tire-screeching U-turn, and peeled out of the drive. Just as they neared Bedford Road,

Bess let out a faint shriek and pointed to a clump of bushes at the end of the drive.

Nancy gasped. Jumping over the bushes and onto the drive directly in front of her car were two figures. In the beam of the headlights, the girls could see that they were men, dressed in black jumpsuits of some kind. One was hefting a long-barreled pistol. The other was unslinging a rifle from his shoulder.

Instinctively Nancy moved her foot onto the brake pedal. But then she stopped. "What am I doing?" she said. "If they think I'm going to slow down and make small talk while a gun is pointed at me, they're crazy!"

Nancy moved her foot back to the gas pedal and stepped on it, mashing down on the horn at the same time. Bess put her hands over her eyes, but George and Nancy saw the two men hold their pose—legs wide apart, guns at the ready—for about two seconds. Then, as the Mustang bore down on them, they jumped aside. Wheels spinning and gravel flying, the car swerved sharply onto Bedford Road.

"Are we going to live?" Bess asked.

"Not if we don't hurry," Nancy answered. "Look."

Behind them, turning out of the private drive and coming fast, was a dark-colored, unmarked van.

"It's not over yet," Nancy said. "Let's see how far they're willing to go."

Except for Nancy's car and the van, Bedford Road was nearly deserted. Nancy raced the car past other estates, past the high school, past a solitary jogger in white. The van stayed close behind, not losing an inch.

Suddenly Nancy saw a traffic light ahead of her. It was green, and Nancy eased up on the gas pedal.

"What are you doing?" Bess cried. "They'll catch us!"

"Maybe, maybe not." Nancy slowed as much as possible, keeping her eyes on the traffic light. Behind them, the van's headlights were bright enough to read by. The light changed to amber and Nancy felt a jolt as the van rammed into the back of her car.

George's head snapped back as the van once again made contact with the Mustang. "Uh, Nancy," she said, "if you're going to do what I think you're going to do, do it now. The light's been yellow for five seconds."

"Right. Hang on!" Nancy pushed the gas pedal and raced through the intersection just after the light turned red. The van's brakes screeched, but then its driver decided to risk running a light. It tore through the intersection only a few feet behind the Mustang.

Nancy shook her head in disbelief. "Where are the police when you really need them?" she joked. Actually, she was glad that a police car hadn't been lurking at the intersection. A high-speed chase through the streets of Bedford might get the driver of the van in trouble. But when he showed his diplomatic papers or whatever he carried around with him, he'd be off the hook. Then Nancy could do one of two things—blow her cover or get arrested. Neither choice was very appealing.

Reluctantly Nancy slowed the car to a respectable speed. "Anybody got any suggestions?" she asked.

Bess spoke up immediately. "Let's eat."

"Oh, Bess," George said with a moan. "Get serious, will you? There's a lunatic on our tail."

"I *am* serious," Bess protested. "There's a pizza place just ahead on the right, and it looks jammed. Do you really think those creeps would follow us in there?"

"I'm ready to try anything," Nancy said, and swerved sharply into the parking lot of Guido's Pizza. As she squeezed the car into the last available space, she glanced into the rearview mirror. The van slowed for a moment, then sped down the block and out of sight.

"It worked," she said, with a shaky laugh. "You were right, Bess. I guess it would have blown their image if they'd followed us to Guido's and shot us over a pepperoni pie."

"Speaking of pepperoni," Bess said, "I really am starving."

"So am I," Nancy agreed. "Let's go pig out."

Guido's was jammed, as Bess had predicted,

but the three girls managed to find a table near the kitchen door. As Nancy sank into a chair, she glanced around and saw several kids from Bedford High, including Carla Dalton. *Terrific,* she thought, *Carla's a quick way to ruin an appetite.* Carla was talking to somebody whose back was to Nancy. She was so involved in whatever she was saying that she didn't notice anyone else.

When their pizza arrived, Nancy discovered that not even Carla Dalton could kill her appetite. Hungrily, she and Bess and George wolfed down slices of the big pie, not saying much of anything. When only one slice was left, Nancy leaned back in her chair and sipped her Coke. "Well, we finally know what Daryl's secret is," she said quietly, "and it's a lot worse than shoplifting."

Bess nodded. "It's really unbelievable, though. I mean, a high-school kid involved in spying? Who would ever guess?"

"That was probably the point," George said. "But Daryl's not the worst one. That man from the defense plant and probably one of the diplomats—they're the real bad guys."

"Daryl's not squeaky clean, though," Nancy remarked. "I'm sure he knew exactly what he was doing." She wasn't really shocked anymore, just angry. And she was more angry at herself than at Daryl. If only she hadn't been so stupid, such an easy mark for Daryl's charms! If she'd kept her mind on her job and her hands to herself, she wouldn't be feeling like such a sucker.

First things first, she told herself. *Solve the case. Then you can kick yourself for being such a dummy!*

Bess broke into her thoughts. "What kind of stuff do you think Daryl was taking from the guy at the defense plant? Blueprints? Secret designs for bombs?"

"Probably," Nancy said. "And I'll bet it paid really well." Well enough, she figured, to keep gas in Daryl's Porsche and a grin on his face. "Daryl did it for the money, I'm sure, not for any political reason."

"I guess it beat bagging groceries after school," George commented. "Daryl must have thought he had it made."

"He did, until Jake found out," Nancy said. "It must have freaked him out, but he was so cool, you would never have guessed. What an actor!" Had Daryl been acting with her, too? she wondered. Coming on to her just so she wouldn't suspect him? She had to admit that that was exactly what he'd done, and she'd fallen for it! Well, she'd stopped falling, and now her eyes were wide open. "What I have to find out," she told the other two, "is who killed Jake. Was it someone from the compound or the man at the defense plant? Or was it Daryl? Or Hal or Walt or Connie?"

"Do you really think Daryl could have done something like that?" Bess asked.

"I'm just not sure," Nancy admitted. "But I have to find out. The question is how? I can't just walk up and—" she broke off suddenly.

"What is it?" George asked.

"Look who's here." Nancy pointed to Carla Dalton's table. Carla and the person she'd been with had stood up and were threading their way through the crowded room. Carla's companion was Brenda Carlton. They were headed toward Nancy.

"What's the ace reporter doing here?" George wondered.

"She'd better not be following me," Nancy said grimly. "We made a deal. If she messes me up, I'll take her reporter's notebook and burn it."

"Who's she with?" Bess asked.

"Oh, that's the famous Carla Dalton." Nancy laughed. "The one who likes to let people fall off trampolines." She giggled and then whispered, "I wonder what she'd say if she knew her ex-boyfriend was a spy?"

"She'd probably chew him out for being stupid enough to get caught," Bess joked.

As Brenda and Carla approached the girls' table, Brenda gave Nancy a sideways glance and a nasty wink. Nancy felt like throwing the last slice of pizza at her and watching the tomato sauce ooze down Brenda's black suede boots, but she held herself back.

Carla was chattering away about Bedford High's big dance as she and Brenda walked by, but she took the time to jostle the girls' table hard enough to spill Nancy's Coke.

Bess took a wad of napkins out of the container and handed them to Nancy. "Carla doesn't give up, does she?" she said, seething. "I don't understand why you haven't gotten back at her."

But Nancy had other things on her mind. Brenda, for one. *Had* she been following them? If she had, Nancy would have to be super careful. The case was at its trickiest point. She couldn't afford to let Brenda's nose for news get even a whiff of what was going on.

Then there was Daryl Gray. How was she going to handle him? "Of course!" she said suddenly. "Carla just gave me the answer."

"The answer to what?" George asked.

"How to get Daryl to spill his guts," Nancy told her. "Bess, you said Alan Wales is playing at the dance tomorrow night, right? So you'll be there, won't you?"

"Of course," Bess said dreamily. "I'm his biggest fan."

"Good, I might need your help." Nancy turned to George. "Yours, too."

"But I don't have a date."

"I've got one for you."

"I don't like blind dates," George protested.

"Trust me," Nancy said with a grin. "You'll love the guy I have in mind."

"So how are you going to handle Daryl?" Bess wanted to know.

"Very carefully," Nancy said. "But no matter what, tomorrow night, I'm going to pop the question to him. Only it won't be one he's expecting."

Chapter

Fourteen

Bᴇss sᴍᴏᴏᴛʜᴇᴅ ᴏᴜᴛ the skirt of her cherry-red dress and stood on tiptoe, trying to get a glimpse of herself in the mirror. "It's no use," she said with a sigh. "I'll have to wait until this place clears out."

"I'm not in any hurry anyway," Nancy said tensely. She and George and Bess were in the girls' bathroom just outside the Bedford High gym. It was the night of the high school's first big dance. For an hour and a half Nancy had been putting on an act—first when Daryl had picked her up at home, then on the drive to Bedford, and for the past forty-five minutes while she'd been dancing with him. She'd laughed and joked and made conversation, pretending that everything was the same between them. She probably deserved an Oscar for her performance, she told herself wryly. But staying in character was growing difficult. She'd been glad when the band had finally taken a break and she could take refuge in the bathroom and just be herself.

"Well, it won't be much longer," she said with a nervous glance at her watch. "I wish my hands weren't so clammy."

"Don't worry," George told her. "Daryl will just think you're excited to be with him."

"Speaking of that," Bess said, giggling, "what do you think of Alan Wales, Nancy? Isn't he absolutely gorgeous?"

"Incredible," Nancy agreed. Actually, she hadn't paid much attention to Bess's new heart-throb, but she didn't want to hurt her friend's feelings. "When this case is over, we'll all have to do something together."

"Oh, sure, that'll be great!" Bess said. "Of course, Alan's really serious about making it in the music business, so he's always busy. But we'll try to find a spare hour somewhere."

Nancy was glad Bess had a new boyfriend, but she just couldn't work up any enthusiasm for the subject, not at the moment, anyway. It wouldn't be long before she had to confront

Daryl, and that prospect was making her heart pound so hard it almost drowned out the sound of Bess's voice.

A girl behind Nancy finally moved away from the mirror, and Nancy grabbed the space. *Well, you don't look terrified,* she told herself. Actually, she looked good. She was wearing a dress she'd worn the year before, at a university dance with Ned—a soft blue wraparound that hugged her waist and came to a mildly revealing V in the front.

That V had put a sparkle in Daryl's eyes, but Nancy knew that the sparkle would fade fast once she started talking to him about Jake Webb, a man at a defense plant, and a diplomatic compound. What worried her was what would happen next. If Daryl was the murderer, would he turn on her? It was hard to imagine his getting vicious, but she knew it was a chance she had to take.

Nancy leaned close to the mirror to touch up her lipstick, and just as she brought the tube to her mouth, a girl moved into the space next to her, bumping Nancy's arm with her elbow.

Nancy stared at the pale red smear on the side of her mouth, and then at the girl who'd helped put it there. Carla Dalton.

George passed Nancy a tissue. Bess raised her eyebrows and shook her head. Nancy wiped her mouth and started over again. Carla ignored everyone, brushed her hair, and then turned to leave.

Suddenly there was a loud shriek, followed by a distinct thud. Carla was sitting on the bathroom floor, skinny legs sticking out in front of her, narrow lips pressed into a thin line of disgust.

Nancy was trying to figure out how Carla had gotten there, not that she cared, when Bess cried out, "Oh, I'm *so* sorry!" Her voice dripped with mock sympathy. "Me and my big feet! My mother always told me to be sure to keep my feet out of the way or people would trip on them, but I guess I just didn't see you coming." She shook her head and clicked her tongue. "Here, let me give you a hand up."

"Don't bother," Carla said through clenched teeth. "You've done enough!" She got clumsily to her feet and stalked out of the bathroom, but not before Nancy saw a large, soapy water stain smack on the rear of Carla's peach colored dress.

"Nice work. Thanks," Nancy whispered to Bess.

"Well, I just couldn't let her keep dumping on you," Bess giggled. "You've got enough on your mind."

George fluffed out her short dark curls and then checked her watch. "It's almost time," she said. "The band'll be back in just a couple of minutes."

Nancy took a deep breath. "You guys know what you're supposed to do, right?"

George nodded. "Don't worry. We'll be there." She grinned. "By the way, you were right about that date you got for me. He's terrific."

"I kind of like him myself," Nancy agreed with a laugh. "Okay, then," she went on. "I'll see you after the next break. Keep your fingers crossed." With another deep breath and a last look in the mirror, she walked out of the bathroom and into the Bedford High gym.

The band was just reassembling, and Nancy took a moment to try to relax before finding Daryl. The gym was decorated with hundreds of crepe-paper streamers, and colored spotlights sent shafts of red, blue, and orange to the floor. Nancy spotted Walt Hogan, looking happier than she'd ever seen him. She didn't see Hal or Connie, and she realized that Connie probably never went to dances. *Maybe when this case is over,* Nancy thought, *Connie will straighten her life out and stop trying so desperately to be somebody she's not.*

Alan Wales, the latest love of Bess's life, picked up his electric guitar and, with a frown of concentration, started in on a wild, pounding rock number that put everyone into motion.

"Okay, Daryl," Nancy said under her breath, "here I come, ready or not."

Her heart still pounding, Nancy threaded her

way through the crowded gym until she reached
Daryl Gray's side. Without a word, Daryl
grabbed her hand and pulled her close to him.

"Hey," Nancy joked, "this is a fast dance. I
don't think I can move like this."

"Who wants to move?" Daryl whispered in
her ear.

"I know what you mean." Nancy traced his
lips with her finger and pretended to be feeling
as passionate as Daryl was. "Let's just stick
around a little while longer, though, okay? If
we leave now, everybody will know why."

"I don't care about everybody," Daryl said
with a grin. "But all right. As long as we're
here, we might as well dance."

For almost half an hour, Nancy danced with
Daryl. The band was good, keeping up a steady
stream of popular rock numbers, as well as a
few originals. They were all loud and fast, and it
was almost impossible to carry on a conversation. Nancy was just as glad. She'd have to do
some fast talking soon enough.

Finally, just before the next break, the band
started in on a dreamy slow dance. Daryl took
Nancy in his arms and held her tight, barely
moving to the music. With a sigh he said, "This
has to be the best night I've ever had."

This is it, Nancy told herself. She pulled her
head back until she could look in Daryl's eyes.
Touching his lips again, she whispered, "It
could be a whole lot better, though, couldn't it?

Especially if we spent some time alone together. I've danced enough now. How about you?"

With a slow smile Daryl laced his fingers through hers and led her through the gym, around the slow-dancing couples, and out the door.

Nancy shivered as they crossed the parking lot, but it wasn't because of the cool night air. It was because the dangerous part of the evening was coming up, when Nancy would find out who Daryl Gray really was. Was he a nice guy gone wrong, or was he a killer?

Except for a few widely spaced lampposts, the Bedford High parking lot was dark, as Nancy had expected. Daryl's Porsche loomed like a black hulk in the shadows. Nancy forced herself to smile as Daryl unlocked the car and ushered her inside. As he walked around to the driver's door, she heard strains of music coming from the gym, and wished, for a second, that she were still at the dance.

Once Daryl got in the car, though, Nancy didn't have time to think of anything but his arms. They were around her immediately, and Nancy couldn't help remembering that just a few days before, she'd loved that feeling. She didn't love it anymore, but even as Daryl held her, she felt a pang of regret that such a gorgeous guy was involved in something so rotten.

Thinking of what Daryl had done, and might

have done, made Nancy pull away. "Hey," she said breathlessly. "Not so fast, there's plenty of time."

"I know, I know." Daryl was just as breathless. "I just love the way you feel." He leaned forward to kiss her.

Nancy put her arms around his neck, and when the kiss was over, she decided it was time. Bringing her lips close to his ear, she whispered softly, "I thought you'd like to know—I found out why Jake Webb was killed."

Chapter
Fifteen

FOR A SECOND Daryl didn't move, and Nancy wondered if he'd even heard her. "Daryl?" she whispered again.

Finally, slowly, Daryl pulled away from her and sat back. In the faint light Nancy could see a look of surprise on his face. But fear was mixed with that surprise, and she knew that nothing was ever going to be the same between them again.

"Well," Daryl said. "Good work, Detective. How'd you do it?"

"I was lucky," Nancy admitted. "A piece of evidence was right in front of me, but I didn't see it for a while. It was on the tape."

"The tape? Jake's tape?" Daryl asked sharply.

"The one and only."

"Wow, you never know, do you?" Daryl gave a low whistle. "So which one did it?"

What an actor, Nancy thought. "It wasn't Hal or Connie," she told him. "It wasn't Walt Hogan, either." That was a guess on Nancy's part.

Daryl frowned. "But I thought you said you knew who killed Jake."

"No, I didn't. I said I knew *why* he was killed. There's a big difference."

Daryl shifted impatiently. "He was killed because he was blackmailing people and one of them finally stood up to him. We already know that."

"Yeah, that's true," Nancy agreed. "But it wasn't one of those three. They were all tucked in their beds when Jake took that fall." Nancy was still going on guesswork. For all she knew, Hal, Connie, and Walt could have formed a team and pushed Jake down the stairs on the count of three. But she didn't believe it, not for a minute. "So," she went on, "don't you want me to tell you what I found?"

"It's not exactly what I had in mind when we came out here," Daryl said, trying to joke, "but if you really want to talk instead of . . . doing other things, then go ahead."

"Okay, here's what I saw on the tape," Nancy said. "I call it 'The Daryl Gray Show.'" Calmly and quietly she went on to describe exactly what she and Bess and George had seen after Daryl had left her house that afternoon. "*Surprised* doesn't even come close to the way I felt when that tape ended," she said. "Sick is more like it."

Daryl didn't say anything, so Nancy kept talking. "But I was confused, too. I mean, I still didn't know what Jake had on you. So I decided to find out. I don't have to tell you where I went, do I? Out Route 110 to a U.S. defense plant. Then back to Bedford to a private estate where Russian diplomats hang out—relax, study a lot of top-secret plans from the defense plant, stuff like that."

Nancy shook her head and laughed softly. "I can just imagine how Jake felt when he realized what was going on. He must have thought he was sitting on a gold mine." She leaned forward slightly, and in the semi-darkness, she saw the expression on Daryl's face. He looked resigned, like a trapped animal that knows it can't get free. But like that trapped animal, he also looked angry, ready to strike out at anyone who came close.

For the first time since she'd left the dance with Daryl, Nancy felt she might be in danger. He was so close to her, physically, and she found herself wishing the Porsche were a little more roomy. Some space would be nice just then, the length of a football field, for example.

You're almost finished, she told herself. *Just get it over with.* "I know Jake told you that he'd found out your secret. I don't know how much of your 'salary' you had to fork over to keep him quiet, but that doesn't matter," Nancy said. "It probably didn't even matter to Jake after a while, because Jake decided to go after the bigger fish, didn't he? Which of your 'contacts' did he try to blackmail? The one at the defense plant? The one here in Bedford? Both?"

Daryl turned his head to look at her, and Nancy saw that the anger was growing stronger. "Well, it doesn't matter," she said. "I'll find out." She spoke quickly, wanting to finish before Daryl exploded. "What I really want to know—and what I think you can tell me—is who killed Jake. Was it you?"

The explosion came then. Nancy felt Daryl's hand—the touch of which had once made her quiver with excitement—close over her wrist in a painfully tight grip. Then he was getting out of the car, dragging her roughly after him. Nancy stumbled and felt her knee scrape the parking lot pavement, but Daryl had grabbed her arms by then, and was pulling her up and pushing her against the car.

"Listen," he whispered hoarsely, "Jake got in over his head, and so have you. If you think I'm a killer, what makes you think I'd stop with Jake Webb?"

Nancy saw the look of desperate fury in Daryl's eyes and knew she needed help. Fortunately she'd planned for it. As she stared back at Daryl, she saw his eyes blink suddenly as three sets of headlights were switched on in three different locations. The glare blinded both of them for a second, but Nancy heard car doors opening and knew that Bess and George were on their way. Most important, George's "blind" date—Ned Nickerson—was with them. Nancy was glad he'd come home for the weekend. Knowing he was there made her feel stronger.

Daryl heard the doors, too, and the sound of hurried footsteps on the pavement. He turned his head just in time to see the three figures moving swiftly toward the Porsche. Then he ran.

"Nan, are you all right?" Bess called out.

"I'm fine!" Nancy shouted back. She took off after Daryl, but before she'd taken even two steps, she felt someone rush past her. When she saw who it was, she stopped. Ned Nickerson could handle Daryl Gray any day of the week.

Ned's strong legs easily ate up the distance between him and Daryl. As Nancy watched he sprang into the air, landed on Daryl's back, and brought them both crashing to the ground. Then he was up, yanking Daryl to his feet. He half-dragged him back to the Porsche and slammed him up against its side.

"Ned!" Nancy had never seen him act so rough. When he'd arrived earlier, she'd told him everything about Daryl, except for his feelings about her—and vice versa. She was saving that for later, when the case was all cleared up. But seeing the tension in Ned's face, she wondered if he suspected something. She hoped not. She definitely couldn't handle it at the moment.

But then Ned loosened his grip on Daryl's jacket and turned to Nancy with an apologetic smile. "Sorry," he said. "I tend to get carried away when some killer threatens my girl-friend."

"Girlfriend!" Daryl exclaimed. Then he cried, "I'm not a killer!"

"You could have fooled me," Ned said quietly, as he stepped away from Daryl and let Nancy take over.

"You didn't kill Jake Webb?" Nancy asked.

Daryl shook his head. "I just said that stuff to scare you off." His voice was drained of energy. He looked like a whipped puppy. "The guy at the defense plant—Mitch Dillon—killed Jake. He told me so." Daryl took a shaky breath and then went on. "See, Jake wasn't satisfied with blackmailing just me. So he forced me to get him in touch with Mitch. Mitch played along with him, let Jake set up a meeting at the

126

school. Then he told Jake to give him the tape or he'd kill him." Daryl shook his head again, as if he couldn't quite believe it. "I don't have to tell you what happened then."

"Knowing Jake, he probably laughed at the guy," Nancy said.

"Yeah, and he died laughing, the stupid jerk." Daryl was calmer now. There was no anger in his voice, just sadness. "Anyway, when Mitch didn't get the tape he was ready to explode. He told me to get it, came on really strong with all kinds of threats."

"It was you in the video lab that day, wasn't it?" Nancy asked.

Daryl nodded. "I started to chase you," he explained, "but I just couldn't go through with it. I mean, what was I supposed to do when I caught you? Beat you up?" He smiled weakly and shrugged. "Waiting until you told me about the tape was one of the hardest times I've ever been through. But then when I watched it with you, I wasn't on it. I thought I could put this whole thing behind me."

Finally Nancy had the entire story. She should have felt like celebrating, but she didn't. She felt more like crying. From the looks on Bess's and George's faces, she could tell they felt the same way. How could you celebrate when someone—even a creep like Jake Webb— had been murdered? When Daryl Gray's life was probably ruined?

Nancy glanced at Ned. As usual, he sensed how she felt before she had to tell him. He came over and put his arm around her shoulders. Nancy smiled at him and then turned back to Daryl.

"I don't think you'll ever be able to put it behind you," she told him. "Not completely, anyway. You'll have to face up to what you've done, and to what the government will want to do to you."

Daryl didn't bother to answer. He just gave a defeated shrug, not meeting her eyes.

"But I think I know a way for you to make it a whole lot easier on yourself," Nancy went on.

Daryl raised his head, a spark of interest in his beautiful eyes. "How?"

"By helping us catch the murderer."

"You've got to be kidding! Mitch has nothing to lose at this point." Daryl's eyes swept over the parking lot, as if he were trying to find an escape route. But he was trapped, and he knew it. "Don't you understand?!" he screamed. "He'll kill me!"

Chapter

Sixteen

NED TURNED THE car smoothly onto Bedford Road, heading toward the high school. Then he glanced over at Nancy, who was frowning in concentration. "Do you really think Mitch Dillon would kill Daryl?"

"I just don't know," Nancy admitted. "Who can say for sure?" She felt uncomfortable just thinking about it. On Friday night, in the parking lot, she'd spent almost forty-five minutes convincing Daryl to see things her way. By helping her put Mitch Dillon behind bars, she'd said, Daryl would be easing his conscience. And it might help him out of some of the trouble he'd gotten himself into. She'd told

Daryl that *he* didn't have much to lose, either. It had been easy enough to say then, when she was persuading Daryl to go along with her plan.

But Monday was three days later, and in a few short hours, they'd be putting that plan into action. It was a good plan, Nancy knew, but no plan was foolproof. And if something went wrong, Daryl would be the one to pay the price.

Sensing her worry, Ned reached over and squeezed her hand. His classload was light for the next few days and he'd decided to stay and help out. "Hey," he said gently. "Everything's going to be fine. I'll be there. George and Bess and Alan will be there. Even the police are coming. And you're way ahead of the game, where they're concerned. You've already solved the case and they're still scratching their heads about it."

"Well, I had a head start on them, plus a very important piece of evidence." Nancy began to feel better. "Besides, I do need them. They're the only ones who can make an arrest."

Nancy giggled, remembering the look on the police captain's face when she'd told him her story. He'd never heard of Nancy Drew, girl detective, and it took two phone calls—one to her father and one to Mr. Parton—to make him stop looking angry and start looking amazed.

Once he got over his amazement, though, the captain had been more than willing to go along with Nancy's plan. It was a simple plan, really.

Daryl had called Mitch Dillon, told him he had the incriminating tape, and set up a meeting with him for Monday afternoon at five-thirty. At the meeting Daryl would make sure that Mitch talked about murdering Jake Webb. The best part of the plan was that Nancy and her friends were going to get the confession on videotape, using a hidden camera.

As Ned drove toward Bedford High, Nancy checked her watch. In a few hours the case would be over, she hoped. The thought of having to wait out the entire day in school was driving her crazy. But she wanted to keep an eye on Daryl and make sure he didn't bolt. She didn't think he would, but she couldn't take that chance.

"Now, remember," Ned joked as he pulled the car to a stop, "don't lose your lunch money and don't cut any classes."

"Very funny," Nancy said. "How about if we trade places? You go to school and I'll scout around the meeting place?"

"No, thanks. But I will make a deal with you." Ned leaned over and put his hand on the back of her neck. "You behave in school and our trip to the mountains will be next weekend. Mom and Dad are dying to get up there. The cabin has a big stone fireplace, and it's really cozy on cold nights."

"You've got yourself a date!" Nancy bent her head and kissed Ned, wondering how she'd ever thought Daryl Gray was exciting. But she had, and she was going to have to deal with that sooner or later. Later, she told herself. She gave Ned another lingering kiss, then hopped out of the car and went in to school.

If Nancy really had been a student, she would have flunked out for sure. At least ten times that day, she'd been caught staring out the window instead of taking notes, and her English teacher had come right out and asked her if she'd left her brains at home. "Where is your mind, Miss Drew?" Nancy was tempted to tell him that her mind was on blackmail, espionage, and murder, but she kept her mouth shut. He would probably have sent her straight to the school psychologist.

She saw Daryl twice—in the hallway and in the cafeteria—and he seemed fine. Nervous, but ready to go, he said. Nancy was nervous, too, and edgy with waiting, but knowing that Daryl was holding up okay made her relax a little.

The next time she saw him was at the meeting place, a public park near Bedford High. She'd joined Ned, Bess, Alan, and George there as soon as school was out. Ned had been exploring the park most of the afternoon, finding the best place to conceal the camera. He was showing Nancy some heavy shrubs that looked perfect, when Daryl came running up to them. Nancy glanced at his face and felt her heart begin to sink. Daryl looked terrified.

"It's Mitch, he . . ." Daryl gasped for breath. "He called me at school, pretended he was my father. We—we can't go through with this!"

"Why not?" Nancy asked. "What did he say?"

"He said he can't make it at five-thirty," Daryl told her. "I don't know if he suspects anything, but he's going to be here in ten minutes, and there's no time to let the police in on the change of plans!"

Nancy felt a moment of panic herself, but in just a few seconds, that panic changed to anger. "Look," she said, "maybe he does suspect something, he wouldn't be a very good spy if he didn't keep his eyes open. But he can't possibly have any idea about what we've got in store for him. We can't just give up. He could be planning to leave the country or something. This might be our last chance to get him!"

"Nancy's right," Ned said quietly. "Besides, if Daryl doesn't show, then Mitch will definitely suspect something."

It was too late to try to do any more persuading. Nancy just looked at Daryl, silently urging him to hang in. Daryl stared at the ground a few seconds, considering. Then he raised his head and nodded at Nancy. "Let's go, Detective."

As calmly as if they had an entire police force

waiting in the wings, the six young people took their places. Bess and her rock star-to-be sat close together on one of the park benches, their arms around each other. They didn't have to pretend to be in love, Nancy noticed.

Nancy, Ned, and George concealed themselves behind the shrubs, where they could film the encounter without being seen. Nancy panned the camera over the park, stopping on Daryl for a few moments.

Daryl was sitting on another bench, some distance away from the young lovers. Nancy had been worried about him before, but as she looked at him now, the worry vanished. He was lounging casually on the bench, idly scanning one of his school books, looking as calm and relaxed as the day she'd first seen him at the stoplight in Bedford.

"He's pretty cool," George commented softly.

Nancy nodded. "He really missed his calling. He should have been an actor." A branch was poking her in the ear; she reached up to push it away and felt Ned's hand close over hers. She smiled and started to say something, but just then Ned's eyes shifted from her face and she felt him tense. "Company," he whispered.

Through the camera lens, Nancy watched a heavyset man stroll into the park. He was wearing jeans and a dark-blue windbreaker, and as he stopped by the duck pond, he brought out a handful of popcorn from his pocket and threw it into the water. He didn't hurry or glance around. He was simply a man taking a late-afternoon walk through the park.

Just one thing set him apart and made Nancy's hands begin to sweat—his bushy mustache. It was the same mustache she'd seen on Jake's tape, and he was the same man who'd met Daryl in front of the defense plant. It was Mitch Dillon, spy, killer, and soon-to-be convicted criminal, if everything went the way Nancy hoped it would.

Dillon stopped feeding the ducks, and as he walked along the curved path at the edge of the pond, Nancy could tell that he wasn't as oblivious to his surroundings as most people would have thought. His eyes roved constantly over the park, looking for signs of a trap. As he glanced over the shrubs where the camera crew was hidden, Nancy instinctively held her breath, even though she knew he couldn't see her.

Then Dillon took a drink from the water fountain, and when he straightened up, he gave the surroundings one last look. Seemingly satisfied, he wiped his mustache and began a slow amble toward Daryl.

Nancy gripped the camera tightly, holding it steady as Dillon eased himself down on the bench beside his "contact." Nancy saw Dillon's lips move; then Daryl nodded, reached into his

135

bookbag, and pulled out a bulky envelope. It wasn't the incriminating tape, of course; it was blank. Daryl didn't hand it over right away, though; instead, he started talking, and Nancy knew he was talking about Jake Webb.

Keep talking, she urged Daryl silently. *Get that murder confession out of Dillon and onto that mini-cassette you're wearing under your shirt.*

Nancy hated being where she was, out of earshot, looking at the scene through a tiny lens. She wanted to be where the action was, hearing everything for herself. It was frustrating, being so out of it. She toyed with the idea of giving the camera to George or Ned and sneaking through the bushes until she was closer to Daryl and Dillon, but she decided it wasn't worth the chance. One false move, one too many twigs snapping under her feet, could blow it. And she couldn't afford to blow it, especially without the police to back her up.

Dillon reached for the envelope then, but Daryl didn't let go. He was still talking. That must have meant that Dillon hadn't said anything about Jake's murder. Nancy wondered why. Could something have gone wrong? Was Daryl being so obvious that Dillon suspected something?

Keeping the camera steady, Nancy looked away from the viewfinder for a second. Maybe a "real" look would tell her something. But before she could see anything, a blinding flash of light went off in the bushes in front of the park bench. Nancy stared long enough to see Mitch Dillon leap up from the bench, the envelope in his hands. Then she dropped the video camera and began running. Something had gone wrong and Dillon was on his feet. Nancy had to stop him before he got away!

Chapter

Seventeen

As Nancy raced through the bushes a scream rang out, shattering the peaceful silence of the park. There was another scream, and then a woman's voice cried, "What are you doing? Let go of me!"

Although the shrubbery blocked Nancy's view, it didn't matter. She would have known that voice anywhere. It belonged to Brenda Carlton. The "ace" reporter had blown it for Nancy again.

Nancy was so angry she was shaking. Mostly she was angry at herself. She'd made the deal with Brenda, and she should have known better. Brenda couldn't be trusted; she was trouble, right down to the tips of her perfectly manicured nails. Thinking about Brenda made Nancy careless for a second, and a second was all it took. A thick root lay like a snake across the path; Nancy tripped on it and went sprawling face down, right next to the bench where Daryl and Mitch Dillon had been sitting.

"Well, well, who's this?" Dillon said with a sneer. "Another member of the kiddie corps? Get up!" he ordered roughly.

Nancy stood up, quickly appraising the situation. Daryl was standing a few feet from the park bench, Brenda's camera and its flash attachment on the ground in front of him. Dillon had one arm around Brenda's neck, and in his other hand he held a gun. The gun was pointed at Brenda's head.

"Nancy, please," Brenda stammered. "I didn't mean for this to happen. If—if you'd just told me everything, I would have stayed out of your way!"

"You've been following me the whole time, haven't you?" Nancy said.

Brenda nodded dumbly and then winced as Dillon tightened his grip around her throat. Brenda's eyes were terrified, and Nancy couldn't help feeling sorry for her. There was no pity in Mitch Dillon's eyes, though. They were about as compassionate as a shark's. "That's enough chitchat, girls," he said. "It's time to stop playing games."

"This isn't a game," Nancy said.

Dillon eyed her coolly. "You're right, it's not. It's real life and it's going to get rough if you don't do what I say." He shifted his glance to Daryl. "I want that camera," he said, eyeing Brenda's camera on the ground. "You hand it to me and nobody gets hurt. I'll walk out of the park and out of your lives. It'll be like a bad dream."

It already is, Nancy thought. Her mind was racing, trying to figure out what to do. Then suddenly she noticed something—Bess and Alan were close by, but neither Ned nor George had followed her through the shrubs. So Dillon had no way of knowing that they were even around. Nancy knew Ned and George well enough to know that they weren't just standing by, waiting to see what happened. One of them had probably snuck out of the park already and called the police. If Nancy could keep Mitch Dillon talking, keep him from leaving somehow, then there was a chance they could get out of the mess. All she needed was time. "What happens if you don't get the camera?" she asked.

Dillon sighed wearily. "If I don't get the camera, then somebody gets hurt. Do you want to guess who?" He spoke as if Nancy were a child asking annoying questions, and Nancy decided to play along with him.

"Who?" she asked.

"Who do you think?" Brenda cried. "I'm the one he's pointing the gun at! Will you just give him the stupid camera so he'll let me go?!"

"Smart girl," Dillon said. "I suggest you follow her advice, Red."

Nancy hated to be called Red, especially by someone like Dillon. "And if I don't, then you'll kill her, just like you killed Jake Webb, right?" she asked.

"You're catching on fast," Dillon replied. "I already killed one nosy kid. I'm not afraid to kill another. You got it just right."

At least we got the confession, Nancy told herself, *no thanks to Brenda.*

Dillon shifted impatiently. "Now, how about the camera, Red?"

Nancy gritted her teeth. "If you want it so much, why don't you get it yourself? Nobody's stopping you. We're all just a bunch of stupid kids, remember?"

"You may be stupid but I'm not," Dillon said. "You think I don't know what'll happen if I reach for that camera? You'll try to play hero and jump me, and even though I'd win, I just don't have time for a brawl right now."

"I'll bet," Nancy said. "Gotta catch a plane to Russia, right? Back to the U.S.S.R."

"I'm starting to lose my patience." Dillon shook his head in disgust and turned to Daryl. "Okay, buddy. Do your partner one last favor and hand me the camera. Now!"

"Don't do it, Daryl!" Nancy shouted.

"Nancy!" Brenda squeaked. "What are you doing? He's going to kill me!"

"That's right." Dillon was staring at Daryl. "I'm going to kill her if you don't give me that camera in ten seconds. Ten . . . nine . . ."

"Hey." Daryl held out his hands. "Just keep cool, Mitch. I'll give it to you."

"Six . . . five . . ."

Brenda opened her mouth, but no sound came out.

"Four . . ."

Slowly Daryl bent down and took hold of the camera strap. As Dillon reached the count of two, Daryl straightened up and in one quick move swung the heavy camera at Dillon's face. At that same instant the gun went off.

The gunshot set Nancy into motion. She didn't know if Dillon hit anyone, but she hurled herself at him, determined to stop him from doing any more damage. She hit him just below the knees, and as she tried to get a good grip on his jeans, Dillon reached down and took a swing at her. His fist collided with her jaw in a punch that gave her an instant headache.

You really do see stars, Nancy thought. Her ears were ringing and her vision was blurred. It was hard to tell exactly what was going on, but she sensed a lot of movement around her. Then she heard a familiar voice calling to her. "Don't worry, Nancy!" Ned shouted. "The police are on their way!"

Nancy rubbed her eyes and saw Ned and Alan racing together after Mitch Dillon, who was charging across an open field of grass, heading for the sidewalk that bordered the park. He was still clutching the fake tape in one hand, and the camera swung wildly by its strap in the other.

If Dillon had only known that neither the tape nor the camera was going to do him any good, he might have gotten away. But he was determined to take all the "evidence" with him, and it slowed him down. The heavy camera kept banging into his knees. It probably hurt, Nancy thought with satisfaction, which was why Dillon finally broke stride for a few seconds and tried to get a tight grip on the camera itself.

Those few seconds were all it took. As Dillon grappled with the camera, Ned and Alan put on a burst of speed and reached him just as he was about to take off again. First Ned, then Alan leaped on top of Dillon, the three of them rolling over and over until they came to a jarring stop against the base of a water fountain. Dillon wasn't going anywhere for the moment; they had him. Nancy closed her eyes in relief.

When she opened them again, the first person she saw was Brenda Carlton, looking more like a bag lady than a fashion-conscious reporter. Her butter-soft leather boots were covered with mud and grass stains, her red silk blouse was missing two buttons, and a smear of lipstick decorated her chin. She was still sitting where Dillon had tossed her; the gun was right next to her, and every time she looked at it, she sobbed hysterically.

A hundred sarcastic remarks went through Nancy's mind, but before she could decide which one to say, Bess touched her shoulder. "Nan?" Her voice was shaky. "Do you know anything about gunshot wounds?"

"What?" Nancy whirled around to face her friend. "Were you hit?!"

"No, I'm okay," Bess assured her. "It's Daryl."

Daryl Gray was sitting a few feet away from Brenda. His handsome face was pale, and his eyes were full of pain. He was clutching his right shoulder, and even as Nancy looked a bright red stream of blood seeped through his fingers.

"I don't think it's too bad," he said as Nancy crouched beside him. "But it sure does hurt."

He grinned weakly, and Nancy smiled back. "Thank you," she said. "You really came through for us."

"So did this," George said triumphantly. She emerged from the bushes and pointed at the video camera she was carrying. "I got the whole scene on tape, every last bit of it!"

Nancy gave her a thumbs-up signal for victory, and at the same moment she heard a police siren, faint at first, but growing louder by the second. It was all over. They'd done it, and Nancy laughed, barely feeling the pain in her swollen jaw.

Chapter

Eighteen

WHEN NANCY WALKED into Mr. Parton's office the next afternoon, the principal stood up and gave her a smile that seemed to light up the entire room. The confused, worried look had left his eyes, and there was a definite spring in his step as he came around the desk to shake her hand.

"Your father told me you were first-rate," he said, beaming at her. "I'm glad I listened to him."

"Thank you," Nancy said with a laugh. "I'm glad you did, too." She sank into a chair and took the mug of steaming tea Mr. Parton offered her.

"How do you feel?" the principal asked. "I understand you made 'direct contact' with Mitch Dillon's fist."

Nancy touched her jaw. There was a purple bruise on it that her makeup didn't quite cover, but she decided it went with the territory. "It only hurts when I laugh," she joked. "Anyway, it was worth it to see the police handcuffing Mitch Dillon." By the time the police had arrived at the park, all the fight had gone out of Mitch. He'd listened in stony silence as his rights were read to him, but Nancy could see the panic in his eyes. He was finished, and he knew it.

"Murder and espionage." Mr. Parton whistled softly. "Right here in Bedford. If Jake Webb hadn't been so greedy, it might still be going on." He shook his head in amazement. "Well, Dillon won't be busy for a long time, that's for sure."

"What about his foreign contact?" Nancy asked.

"I don't suppose we'll ever get the whole story," Mr. Parton said, "but I heard on the news this morning that two 'diplomats' checked out of their Bedford mansion last night. Mother Russia probably wanted them home fast."

"I guess that takes care of the spy ring, for a while anyway," Nancy said. "What's going to happen to Daryl Gray?"

Mr. Parton's good spirits took a dive for a

moment. "I don't know yet." He sighed. "He's in deep trouble, no doubt about that. I still can't believe he did what he did."

Nancy agreed, but she felt strongly that Daryl deserved a break. "I know you feel terrible about him," she said, "but I think if it hadn't been for Daryl, Mitch Dillon would have escaped yesterday. Daryl did the right thing in the end. He also got shot for it."

Mr. Parton nodded. "You're right. And I'm sure the government will agree with you. He'll have to pay for what he did, but maybe the price won't be so high." He sipped some tea and relaxed again. "By the way, the police are holding Jake's videotape for evidence, but they've promised to keep as quiet as they can about Walt and Hal and Connie."

"That's great!" In spite of what they'd done, Nancy couldn't help feeling that those three kids had been victims as much as anyone else. "Have you talked to them?"

"To all three," Mr. Parton told her. "Hal's taking the SATs again, Walt decided to bench himself for a while, and Connie's agreed to get some help for her shoplifting problem. So there's a happy ending after all. And," he went on, "I didn't mention your part in the case, even though I wanted to."

"Good. Who knows?" Nancy said. "I might have to come here undercover again someday."

Mr. Parton winced and then shook hands with her. "Don't take this the wrong way," he said, "but I hope not!"

As Nancy took a last walk through the halls of Bedford High, there was a spring in her step, too. She had solved the case, but it was more than that. She caught sight of Hal and Walt and Connie and noticed that all three of them seemed to have lightened up overnight. In fact, the whole atmosphere of the school had lightened up. Maybe since the biggest secret had been revealed, the smaller secrets—injury and cheating and shoplifting—could be forgotten.

A lot of kids were carrying copies of *Today's Times,* and Nancy noticed that Brenda Carlton had finally gotten her name on a front-page story, beneath the headline BEDFORD POLICE CRACK ESPIONAGE RING. Nancy smiled to herself as she picked a copy of the discarded paper off the hall floor. Brenda must have been very happy to keep her part of the bargain and leave Nancy's name out of the story.

As Nancy quickly scanned the article, she saw with relief that Daryl's part in helping catch Dillon got just as much play as his role of courier for spies. Brenda, naturally, didn't mention her own near-disastrous actions at all.

Daryl was still in the hospital, the story said, but was expected to recover quickly. Nancy had a feeling that he could always bounce back, and she was sure that in a few years he'd get over the nightmare he'd been involved in.

So things were turning out okay, she thought as she pushed open the door and walked outside. She had just one loose end to tie up, and then she could put the Bedford High case behind her and move on to the next one, whatever it might be.

The "loose end" was Ned Nickerson, and he was waiting for her in his car. *This is as good a time as any to tell him about Daryl,* Nancy thought. She pulled her jacket collar up against the chilly October wind and went down the steps to meet him.

"Hi!" Ned pushed open the door for her and took her hand as she slid in. "Did everything go okay?"

"Fine," Nancy said, and told him what Mr. Parton had told her.

"Great. Then it's all over, huh?"

"Almost." Nancy linked her fingers with his and took a deep breath. She wished she'd had a chance to discuss her problem with Bess, but there hadn't been time. Besides, Bess was so involved with Alan Wales that she was hardly paying attention to anything that was going on around her. She and Alan ate, slept, and breathed guitars and musicians. Nancy was on her own. After another deep breath she said,

"Ned, there's something I have to talk to you about."

"I bet I can guess," Ned said softly. "It's Daryl Gray, isn't it?"

"You mean you knew?"

"Not really," Ned told her. "But I saw the way he looked at you a couple of times. And the way you looked at him."

Nancy should have guessed. Ned knew her better than anyone else. "It wasn't much, really. I mean we didn't fall in love or anything like that. I guess we were just attracted to each other. I wasn't looking for it to happen, it just did."

"You don't have to explain," Ned said. He stared ahead of him, at the entrance to Bedford High.

"But I want to!" Nancy squeezed his hand and tried to get him to look at her. "I feel terrible telling you, but it's better than keeping it from you. Because I love you," she said. "No other guy could be as perfect for me as you are."

"Then it's over?" Ned asked.

"It hardly got started," Nancy said.

"So there's nothing to talk about, is there?" Ned finally looked at her, but Nancy couldn't read the expression in his eyes. She couldn't tell what he was thinking.

"I guess not," she said. "But I wanted to tell you anyway."

"I understand. I'm glad you did." Ned pulled her close and kissed her gently. "Let's get out of here, okay?"

"Okay!" Nancy kissed him back and settled herself in the seat. She was glad she'd told him, too, but had she done the right thing? Ned said he understood, but did he, really? Would she have understood if he'd told her about some girl at the university?

Nancy shook her head, trying to get rid of such disturbing thoughts. It was over. She'd done what she thought was right, and she'd just have to wait to see what happened.

As the car pulled away from the school, Nancy turned and took one last look. It was a handsome, modern building, and it appeared peaceful in the afternoon sun. It was hard to believe the things that had gone on behind its red brick walls.

Nancy turned and caught Ned's eye. He was smiling at her and she felt a sudden urge to run her fingers through his hair. She also felt relieved that she'd told him the truth about Daryl. She didn't want any secrets between her and Ned. She'd found enough secrets at Bedford High.

Nancy's next case:

When she investigates a rock star's mysterious disappearance, Nancy once again finds herself probing perilous secrets! Her only lead takes her straight to Bess's new boyfriend. What is he hiding? Finding out may kill her friendship with Bess. But *not* finding out may kill the kidnapped rock star—with Nancy and her friends next on the hit list.

Can Nancy survive the dark side of the rock scene? Find out in *DEADLY INTENT*—Case #2 in *The Nancy Drew Files*,™ available now.

HAVE YOU SEEN
NANCY
DREW®
LATELY?

Nancy Drew has become a girl of the 80's! There is hardly a girl from seven to seventeen who doesn't know her name.

Now you can continue to enjoy Nancy Drew in a new series, written for older readers—THE NANCY DREW FILES.™ Each pocket-sized book has more romance, fashion, mystery and adventure.

THE NANCY DREW FILES™

- # 1 SECRETS CAN KILL 64193/$2.75
- # 2 DEADLY INTENT 64393/$2.75
- # 3 MURDER ON ICE 84194/$2.75
- # 4 SMILE AND SAY MURDER 62557/$2.50
- # 5 HIT AND RUN HOLIDAY 64394/$2.75
- # 6 WHITE WATER TERROR 63020/$2.50
- # 7 DEADLY DOUBLES 62543/$2.75
- # 8 TWO POINTS FOR MURDER 63079/$2.75
- # 9 FALSE MOVES 63076/$2.75
- # 10 BURIED SECRETS 63077/$2.75

JOIN NANCY DREW
AT THE COUNTRY CLUB!

You can be a charter member of Nancy Drew's River Heights Country Club™— Join today! Be a part of the wonderful, exciting and adventurous world of River Heights, USA™.

You'll get four issues of the Country Club's quarterly newsletter with valuable advice from the nation's top experts on make-up, fashion, dating, romance, and how to take charge and plan your future. Plus, you'll get a complete River Heights, USA, Country Club™ membership kit containing an official ID card for your wallet, an 8-inch full color iron-on transfer, a laminated bookmark, 25 sticker seals, and a beautiful enamel pin of the Country Club logo.

It's a retail value of over $12. But, as a charter member, right now you can get in on the action for only $5.00. So, fill out and mail the coupon and a check or money order now. *Please do not send cash.* Then get ready for the most exciting adventure of your life!

— —

MAIL TO: Nancy Drew's River Heights Country Club
House of Hibbert   CN-4609
Trenton, NJ 08650

Here's my check or money order for $5.00! I want to be a charter member of the exciting new Nancy Drew's River Heights, USA Country Club™.

Name _____ Age _____

Address _____

City _____ State _____ ZIP _____

Allow six to eight weeks for delivery.   ·NDDC6